LOIS LOWRY

GATHERING BLUE

HOUGHTON MIFFLIN COMPANY BOSTON

Walter Lorraine Books

Walter Lorraine (wr) Books

Library of Congress Cataloging-in-Publication Data

Lowry, Lois.
Gathering Blue / by Lois Lowry.
p. cm.
Summary: Lamed and suddenly orphaned, Kira is mysteri-
ously removed from her squalid village to live in the palatial
Council Edifice, where she is expected to use her gifts as a
weaver to do the bidding of the all-powerful Guardians.
ISBN 0-618-05581-9
[1. Science fiction.] I. Title.

PZ7.L9673 Gat 2000
[Fic]—dc21   00-024359

Printed in the United States of America
RRD 10 9 8 7 6 5 4 3 2 1

GATHERING BLUE

GATHERING BLUE

1

"Mother?"

There was no reply. She hadn't expected one. Her mother had been dead now for four days, and Kira could tell that the last of the spirit was drifting away.

"Mother." She said it again, quietly, to whatever was leaving. She thought that she could feel its leave-taking, the way one could feel a small whisper of breeze at night.

Now she was all alone. Kira felt the aloneness, the uncertainty, and a great sadness.

This had been her mother, the warm and vital woman whose name had been Katrina. Then after the brief and unexpected sickness, it had become the body of Katrina, still containing the lingering spirit. After four sunsets and sunrises, the spirit, too, was gone. It was simply a body. Diggers would come and sprinkle a layer of soil over the flesh, but even so it would be eaten by the clawing, hungry creatures that came at night. Then the bones would scatter, rot, and crumble to become part of the earth.

Kira wiped briefly at her eyes, which had filled suddenly with tears. She had loved her mother, and would miss her terribly. But it was time for her to go. She wedged her walking stick in the soft ground, leaned on it, and pulled herself up.

She looked around uncertainly. She was young still, and had not experienced death before, not in the small two-person family that she and her mother had been. Of course she had seen others go through the rituals. She could see some of them in the vast foul-smelling Field of Leaving, huddled beside the ones whose lingering spirits they tended. She knew that a woman named Helena was there, watching the spirit leave her infant, who had been born too soon. Helena had come to the Field only the day before. Infants did not require the four days of watching; the wisps of their spirits, barely arrived, drifted away quickly. So Helena would return to the village and her family soon.

As for Kira, she had no family, now. Nor any home. The cott she had shared with her mother had been burned. This was always done after sickness. The small structure, the only home Kira had ever known, was gone. She had seen the smoke in the distance as she sat with the body. As she watched the spirit of her mother drift away, she had seen the cindered fragments of her childhood life whirl into the sky as well.

She felt a small shudder of fear. Fear was always a part of life for the people. Because of fear, they made shelter and found food and grew things. For the same reason, weapons were stored, waiting.

2

There was fear of cold, of sickness and hunger. There was fear of beasts.

And fear propelled her now as she stood, leaning on her stick. She looked down a last time at the lifeless body that had once contained her mother, and considered where to go.

Kira thought about rebuilding. If she could find help, though help was unlikely, it wouldn't take long to build a cott, especially not this time of year, summerstart, when tree limbs were supple and mud was thick and abundant beside the river. She had often watched others building, and Kira realized that she could probably construct some sort of shelter for herself. Its corners and chimney might not be straight. The roof would be difficult because her bad leg made it almost impossible for her to climb. But she would find a way. Somehow she would build a cott. Then she would find a way to make a life.

Her mother's brother had been near her in the Field for two days, not guarding Katrina, his sister, but sitting silently beside the body of his own woman, the short-tempered Solora, and that of their new infant who had been too young to have a name. They had nodded to each other, Kira and her mother's brother, in acknowledgment. But he had departed, his time in the Field of Leaving finished. He had tykes to tend; he and Solora had two others in addition to the one that had brought about her death. The others were still small, their names yet of one syl-

3

lable: Dan and Mar. *Perhaps I could care for them,* Kira thought briefly, trying to find her own future within the village. But even as the thought flickered within her, she knew that it would not be permitted. Solora's tykes would be given away, distributed to those who had none. Healthy, strong tykes were valuable; properly trained, they could contribute to family needs and would be greatly desired.

No one would desire Kira. No one ever had, except her mother. Often Katrina had told Kira the story of her birth — the birth of a fatherless girl with a twisted leg — and how her mother had fought to keep her alive.

"They came to take you," Katrina said, whispering the story to her in the evening, in their cott, with the fire fed and glowing. "You were one day old, not yet named your one-syllable infant name —"

"Kir."

"Yes, that's right: Kir. They brought me food and were going to take you away to the Field —"

Kira shuddered. It was the way, the custom, and it was the merciful thing, to give an unnamed, imperfect infant back to the earth before its spirit had filled it and made it human. But it made her shudder.

Katrina stroked her daughter's hair. "They meant no harm," she reminded her.

Kira nodded. "They didn't know it was *me*."

"It *wasn't* you, yet."

"Tell me again why you told them no," Kira whispered.

Her mother sighed, remembering. "I knew I would not have another child," she pointed out. "Your father had been taken by beasts. It had been several months since he went off to hunt and did not return. And so I would not give birth again.

"Oh," she added, "perhaps they would have given me one eventually, an orphan to raise. But as I held you — even then, with your spirit not yet arrived and with your leg bent wrong so that it was clear you would not ever run — even then, your eyes were bright. I could see the beginning of something remarkable in your eyes. And your fingers were long and well-shaped —"

"And strong. My hands were strong," Kira added with satisfaction. She had heard the story so often; each time of hearing, she looked down at her strong hands with pride.

Her mother laughed. "So strong they gripped my own thumb fiercely and would not let go. Feeling that fierce tug on my thumb, I could not let them take you away. I simply told them no."

"They were angry."

"Yes. But I was firm. And, of course, my father was still alive. He was old then, four syllables, and he had been the leader of the people, the chief guardian, for a long time. They respected him. And your father would have been a greatly respected leader too had he not died on the long hunt. He had already been chosen to be a guardian."

"Say my father's name to me," Kira begged.

Her mother smiled in the firelight. "Christopher," she said. "You know that."

"I like to hear it, though. I like to hear you say it."

"Do you want me to go on?"

Kira nodded. "You were firm. You insisted," she reminded her mother.

"Still, they made me promise that you would not become a burden."

"I haven't, have I?"

"Of course not. Your strong hands and wise head make up for the crippled leg. You are a sturdy and reliable helper in the weaving shed; all the women who work there say so. And one bent leg is of no importance when measured against your cleverness. The stories you tell to the tykes, the pictures you create with words — and with thread! The threading you do! It is unlike any threading the people have ever seen. Far beyond anything I could do!" Her mother stopped. She laughed. "Enough. You mustn't tease me into flattery. Don't forget that you are still a girl, and often willful, and just this morning, Kira, you forgot to tidy the cott even though you had promised."

"I won't forget tomorrow," Kira said sleepily, snuggling against her mother on the raised sleeping mat. She pushed her twisted leg into a more comfortable position for the night. "I promise."

But now there was no one to help her. She had no

family left, and she was not a particularly useful person in the village. For everyday work, Kira helped in the weaving shed, picking up the scraps and leavings, but her twisted leg diminished her value as a laborer and even, in the future, as a mate.

Yes, the women liked the fanciful stories that she told to amuse restless tykes, and they admired the little threadings that she made. But those things were diversions; they were not work.

The sky, with the sun no longer overhead but sending shadows now into the Field of Leaving from the trees and thorn bushes at its edge, told her that it was long past midday. In her uncertainty she had lingered here too long. Carefully she gathered the skins on which she had slept these four nights guarding her mother's spirit. Her fire was cold ashes, a blackened smudge. Her water container was empty and she had no more food.

Slowly, using her stick, she limped toward the path that led back to the village, holding on to a small hope that she might still be welcome there.

Tykes played at the edge of the clearing, scampering about on the moss-covered ground. Pine needles stuck to their naked bodies and in their hair. She smiled. She recognized each little one. There was the yellow-haired son of her mother's friend; she remembered his birth two mid-summers ago. And the girl whose twin had died; she was younger than the yellow-haired one, just toddling, but she giggled and shrieked with the others, playing catch-me-while-

I'm-running. Tussling, the toddlers slapped and kicked at each other, grabbing toy-sticks, flailing with their small fists. Kira remembered watching her childhood companions at such play, preparing for the real scramble of adult life. Unable to participate because of her flawed leg, she had watched from the sidelines with envy.

An older child, a dirty-faced boy of eight or nine years, still too young for puberty and the two-syllable name that he would receive, looked over at her from the place where he was clearing underbrush and sorting the twigs into bundles for firestarting. Kira smiled. It was Matt, who had always been her friend. She liked Matt. He lived in the swampy, disagreeable Fen, probably the child of a dragger or digger. But he ran freely through the village with his disorderly friends, his dog always at his heels. Often he stopped, as now, to do some chore or small job in return for a few coins or a sweet. Kira called a greeting to the boy. The dog's bent tail, matted with twigs and leaves, thumped on the ground, and the boy grinned in reply.

"So you be back from the Field," he said. "What's it like there? Scared, was you? Did creatures come in the night?"

Kira shook her head and smiled at him. Younger, one-syllable tykes were not allowed in the Field, so it was natural that Matt would be curious and a little in awe. "No creatures," she reassured him. "I had fire, and it kept them away."

"So Katrina be gone now from her body?" he asked in his dialect. People from the Fen were oddly different. Always identifiable by their strange speech and crude manners, they were looked down upon by most people. But not by Kira. She was very fond of Matt.

She nodded. "My mother's spirit has gone," she acknowledged. "I watched it leave her body. It was like mist. It drifted away."

Matt came over to her, still carrying an armful of twigs. He squinted at her ruefully and wrinkled his nose. "Your cott is horrid burnt," he told her.

Kira nodded. She knew that her home had been destroyed, though secretly she had hoped she was mistaken. "Yes," she sighed. "And everything in it? My frame? Did they burn my threading frame?"

Matt frowned. "I tried to save things but it's mostly all burnt. Just your cott, Kira. Not like when there's a big sickness. This time it just be your mum."

"I know." Kira sighed again. In the past there had been sicknesses that spread from one cott to the next, with many deaths. When that happened, a huge burning would take place, followed by a rebuilding that became almost festive with the noise of workers smearing wet mud over the fitted wooden sides of new structures, methodically slapping it into smoothness. The charred smell of the burning would remain in the air even as the new cotts rose.

But today there was no festivity. There were only the usual sounds. Katrina's death had changed nothing in the lives of the people. She had been there. Now she was gone. Their lives continued.

With the boy still beside her, Kira paused at the well and filled her container with water. Everywhere she heard arguing. The cadence of bickering was a constant sound in the village: the harsh remarks of men vying for power; the shrill bragging and taunting of women envious of one another and irritable with the tykes who whined and whimpered at their feet and were frequently kicked out of the way.

She cupped her hand over her eyes and squinted against the afternoon sun to find the gap where her own cott had been. She took a deep breath. It would be a long walk to gather saplings and a hard chore to dig the mud by the riverbank. The corner timbers would be heavy to lift and hard to drag. "I have to start building," she told Matt, who still held a bundle of twigs in his scratched, dirty arms. "Do you want to help? It could be fun if there were two of us.

"I can't pay you, but I'll tell you some new stories," she added.

The boy shook his head. "I be whipped iffen I don't finish the fire twiggies." He turned away. After a hesitation, he turned back to Kira and said in a low voice, "I heared them talking. They don't want you should stay. They be planning to turn you out, now your mum be dead. They be set on putting you in the Field for the beasts. They talk about having draggers take you."

Kira felt her stomach tighten with fear. But she

tried to keep her voice calm. She needed information from Matt and it would make him wary to know she was frightened. "Who's 'they'?" she asked in an annoyed, superior tone.

"Them women," he replied. "I heared them talking at the well. I be picking up wood chippies from the refuse, and them didn't even notice me listening. But they want your space. They want where your cott was. They aim to build a pen there, to keep the tykes and the fowls enclosed so they don't be having to chase them all the time."

Kira stared at him. It was terrifying, almost unbelievable, the casualness of the cruelty. In order to pen their disobedient toddlers and chickens, the women would turn her out of the village to be devoured by the beasts that waited in the woods to forage the Field.

"Whose was the strongest voice against me?" she asked after a moment.

Matt thought. He shifted the twigs in his hands, and Kira could see that he was reluctant to get involved in her problems and fearful of his own fate. But he had always been her friend. Finally, looking around first to be certain he wouldn't be overheard, he told her the name of the person with whom Kira would have to do battle.

"Vandara," he whispered.

It came as no surprise. Nonetheless, Kira's heart sank.

2

First, Kira decided, it made sense to pretend she knew nothing. She would go back to the site of the cott where she had lived with her mother and begin to rebuild. Perhaps the simple fact of seeing her there at work would deter the women who hoped to drive her away.

Leaning on her stick, she made her way through the crowded village. Here and there, people acknowledged her presence with a curt nod; but they were busy, all of them at their daily work, and pleasantries were not part of their custom.

She saw her mother's brother. With his son, Dan, he was working in the garden beside the cott where he had lived with Solora and the tykes. Weeds had gone untended while his wife had neared her time, given birth, and died. Then more days had passed, more weeds had flourished, while he sat in the Field with his dead wife and infant. The poles that held beans entwined had toppled, and he was angrily setting them upright as Dan tried to help and the younger tyke, the girl named Mar, sat playing in the dirt at the edge. While Kira looked on, the man slapped his son hard on the shoulder, scolding him for not holding the pole straight.

She walked past them, planting her stick firmly in the ground with each step, planning to nod if they acknowledged her. But the small girl playing in the dirt only whimpered and spat; she had tried tasting some pebbles, in the way of toddlers, and had found herself with a mouthful of foul-tasting grit. The boy Dan glanced at Kira but made no sign of greeting or recognition; he was cringing from his father's slap. The man, her mother's only brother, didn't look up from his labor.

Kira sighed. At least he had help. Unless she could enlist her small friend, Matt, and some of his mates, she would have to do all of her work — rebuilding, gardening — herself, assuming she was allowed to stay.

Her stomach growled, and she realized how hungry she was. Rounding the path past a row of small cotts, she approached her own location and came upon the black heap of ashes that had been her home. There was nothing left of their household things. But she was pleased to see that the little garden remained. Her mother's flowers still bloomed, and the summer-start vegetables were ripening in the sun. For now, at least, she would have some food.

Or would she? As she watched, a woman darted out of a clump of nearby trees, glanced at Kira, and then brazenly began to pull carrots from the garden that Kira and her mother had tended together.

"Stop it! Those are mine!" Kira moved forward as quickly as she could, dragging her deformed leg.

Laughing contemptuously, the woman sauntered away, her hands filled with dirt-encrusted carrots.

Kira hurried to the remains of the garden. She set her water container on the ground, pulled up some tubers, brushed the dirt away, and began to eat. Without a hunter as part of their family, she and her mother had not eaten meat except for the occasional small creature that they could catch within the boundaries of the village. They could not go to the woods to hunt, the way men did. Fish from the river were plentiful and easy to catch, and they felt no need of anything more.

But the vegetables were essential. She was fortunate, she realized, that the garden had not been entirely stripped during her four days in the Field.

Her hunger satisfied, she sat down to rest her leg. She looked around. On the edge of her space, near the ashes, a pile of saplings stripped of their branches was arranged, as if someone had been preparing to help her rebuild.

But Kira knew better. She rose and tentatively picked up one of the slender, pliable saplings from the pile.

Vandara emerged immediately from the nearby clearing where Kira realized she had been waiting and watching. Kira didn't know where the woman lived or who her hubby or children might be. Her cott was none of those nearby. But she was very much known in the village. People whispered about her. She was known, and respected. Or feared.

The woman was tall and muscular, with long, tangled hair pulled back roughly and tied with a thong at the back of her neck. Her eyes were dark, and her direct look pierced any calmness that Kira might have felt. The ragged scar that marked her chin and continued down her neck to her broad shoulder was said to be a remnant of a long-ago battle with one of the forest creatures. No one else had ever survived such a clawing, and the scar reminded everyone of Vandara's courage and vigor as well as her malevolence. She had been attacked and clawed, the children whispered, when she tried to steal an infant creature from its mother's den.

Today, facing Kira, she was once again preparing to destroy someone's young.

Unlike the forest creature, Kira had no claws with which to fight. She gripped her wooden cane tightly and tried to stare back with no hint of fear.

"I've returned to rebuild my cott," she told Vandara.

"Your space is gone. It's mine now. Those saplings are mine."

"I will cut my own," Kira conceded. "But I will rebuild on this space. This was my father's space before I was born, and my mother's after he died. Now that she is dead, it's mine."

Other women emerged from surrounding cotts. "We need it," one called. "We're going to use the

15

saplings to build a pen for the tykes. It was Vandara's idea."

Kira looked at the woman, who was holding the arm of a toddler roughly. "It might be a good idea," Kira replied, "if you want to pen your little ones. But not on this piece of ground. You can build a pen somewhere else."

She saw Vandara lean down and pick up a rock the size of a tyke's fist. "We don't want you here," the woman said. "You don't belong in the village anymore. You're worthless, with that leg. Your mother always protected you but she's gone now. You should go too. Why didn't you just stay in the Field?"

Kira saw that she was surrounded by hostile women who had come from their cotts and were watching Vandara for instructions and leadership. Several, she noticed, had rocks in their hands. If one rock were thrown, others would follow, she knew. They were all waiting for the first.

What would my mother have done? she thought frantically, and tried to call wisdom from the bit of her mother's spirit that lived on in her now.

Or my father, who never knew of my birth? His spirit is in me, too.

Kira straightened her shoulders and spoke. She held her voice steady and tried to meet the eyes of each woman in turn. Some lowered their gaze and looked at the ground. That was good. It meant they were weak.

16

"You know that in a village conflict that could bring death, we must go to the Council of Guardians," Kira reminded them. She heard some murmurs of assent. Vandara's hand still gripped the rock, and her shoulders were tense, preparing to throw.

Kira looked directly at Vandara but she was speaking to the others now, in need of their support. She appealed not to their sympathy, because she knew they had none, but to their fear.

"Remember that if conflict is not taken to the Council of Guardians, and if there is a death . . ."

She heard a murmur. "If there is a death . . ." she heard a woman repeat in an uncertain, apprehensive voice.

Kira waited. She stood as tall and straight as she could.

Finally a woman in the group completed words of the rule. "The causer-of-death must die."

"Yes. The causer-of-death must die." Other voices repeated it. One by one they released the rocks. One by one each woman chose not to be a causer-of-death. Kira began to relax slightly. She waited. She watched.

Finally only Vandara still held her weapon. Glaring, Vandara menaced her, bending her elbow as if to throw. But at last she too dropped the rock on the ground, with a slight harmless toss toward Kira.

"I will take her to the Council of Guardians then," Vandara announced to the women. "I am will-

17

ing to be her accuser. Let *them* cast her out." She laughed harshly. "No need for us to waste a life getting rid of her. By sunset tomorrow this ground can be ours and she will be gone. She will be in the Field, waiting for the beasts."

The women all glanced toward the forest, deep in shadows now: the place where the beasts waited. Kira forced herself not to follow their looks with her own eyes.

With the same hand that had held the rock, Vandara stroked the scar on her throat. She smiled cruelly. "I remember what it was like," she said, "to see your own blood pour upon the ground.

"I survived," she reminded them all. "I survived because of my strength.

"By night-start tomorrow, when she feels the claws at her throat," she went on, "this two-syllable mistake of a girl will wish she had died of sickness beside her mother."

Nodding in agreement, the women turned their backs on Kira and moved away, scolding and kicking at the small tykes by their sides. The sun was low in the sky now. They would attend to their evening tasks, preparing for the return of the village men, who would need food and fire and the wrapping of wounds.

One woman was soon to give birth; perhaps that would happen tonight, and the others would attend her, muffling her cries and assessing the value of the infant. Others would be coupling tonight, creating new people, new hunters for the future of the village as the old ones died of wounds and illness and age.

Kira did not know what the Council of Guardians would decide. She knew only that whether she was to stay or go, to rebuild on her mother's piece of land or to enter the Field and face the creatures who were waiting in the forest, she would have to do it alone. Wearily she sat on the ash-blackened earth to wait for night.

She reached for a nearby piece of wood and turned it over in her hands, measuring its strength and its straightness. For a cott, should she be permitted to stay, she would need some sturdy lengths of solid wood. She would go to the woodcutter named Martin. He had been her mother's friend. She could barter with him, maybe offering to decorate a fabric for his wife, in exchange for the beams she would need.

For her future, for the work with which she thought she might earn her living, she would also need some small, straight pieces of wood. This one was too pliable and would not do, she realized, and dropped it on the ground. Tomorrow, if the Council of Guardians decided in her favor, she would look for the kind of wood she needed: short, smooth pieces she could fit together at the corners. She was already planning to build a new threading frame.

Kira had always had a clever way with her hands. When she was still a tyke, her mother had taught her to use a needle, to pull it through woven fabric and create a pattern with colored threads. But suddenly, recently, the skill had become more than simple cleverness. In one astounding burst of creativity, her ability had gone far beyond her mother's teaching. Now, without instruction or practice, without hesitancy, her fingers felt the way to twist and weave and stitch the special threads together to create designs rich and explosive with color. She did not understand how the knowledge had come to her. But it was there, in her fingertips, and now they trembled slightly with eagerness to start. If only she was allowed to stay.

3

A messenger, bored and scratching at an insect bite on his neck, came to Kira in the dawn and told her that she must report to the Council of Guardians at late morning. When the sun was approaching midday, she tidied herself and went, obedient to his instruction.

The Council Edifice was surprisingly splendid. It remained from before the Ruin, a time so far past that none of the people now living, none of their parents or grandparents, had been born. The people knew of the Ruin only from the Song that was presented at the yearly Gathering.

Rumor said that the Singer, whose only job in the village was the annual presentation of the Song, prepared his voice by resting for days and sipping certain oils. The Ruin Song was lengthy and exhausting. It began with the beginning of time, telling the entire story of the people over countless centuries. It was frightening too. The story of the past was filled with warfare and disasters. Most especially it was frightening when it recalled the Ruin, the end of the civilization of the ancestors. Verses told of smoky, poisonous fumes, of great fractures in the earth itself, of the way huge buildings toppled and were swept away by the seas. All of the people were required to listen each year, but sometimes mothers protectively covered the ears of their smallest tykes during the description of the Ruin.

Very little had survived the Ruin, but somehow the structure called the Council Edifice had remained standing and firm. It was immeasurably old. Several windows still contained patterned glass of deep reds and golds, amazing things, for knowledge of the way of making such remarkable glass had been lost. Some remaining windows, ones in which the colored glass had shattered, were now paned in a thick, ordinary glass that distorted the view through bubbles and ripples. Other windows were simply boarded over, and parts of the building's interior were darkly shadowed. Still, the Edifice was magnificent in comparison to the ordinary sheds and cottages of the village.

Kira, reporting near midday as she had been ordered by the messenger, walked alone down a long hallway lit on either side by sputtering flames from tall sconces fed with oil. She could hear the voices of the meeting ahead, behind a closed door: men's voices in muted arguing. Her stick thumped on the wooden floor and the foot of her flawed leg brushed the boards with a sweeping sound, as if she dragged a broom.

"Take pride in your pain," her mother had

always told her. "You are stronger than those who have none."

She remembered that now and tried to find the pride that her mother had taught her to feel. She straightened her thin shoulders and smoothed the folds of her coarsely woven shift. She had washed carefully in the clear stream water and had cleaned her nails with a sharp twig. She had combed her hair with the carved wooden comb that had been her mother's and which she had added to her own small storage sack after her mother's death. Then she had braided her hair, using her hands to interweave the thick dark strands deftly, tying the end of the heavy plait with a leather strip.

Steadying her apprehensions with a deep breath, Kira knocked on the heavy door to the room where the Council of Guardians' meeting was already in progress. It opened a crack, spilling a wedge of light into the dim hall. A man looked out and eyed her suspiciously. He widened the opening and gestured her inside.

"The accused orphan girl Kira is here!" the door guard announced, and the muttering subsided. In silence they all turned to watch her enter.

The chamber was huge. Kira had been there before, with her mother, on ceremonial occasions like the annual Gathering. Then, they had sat with the crowds on rows of benches, facing the stage that was furnished only with an altar table holding the

Worship-object, the mysterious wooden construction of two sticks connected to form a cross. It was said to have had great power in the past, and the people always bowed briefly and humbly toward it in respect.

But now she was alone. There were no crowds, no ordinary citizens, only the Council of Guardians: twelve men who sat facing her across a long table at the foot of the stage. Rows of oil lamps made the room bright, and each of the men had his personal torch behind him, illuminating stacked and scattered papers that lay on the table. They watched her as she made her way hesitantly up the aisle.

Quickly, remembering the procedure that she had seen at every ceremony, Kira arranged her hands in a reverent position, cupped together, fingertips below her chin, as she arrived at the table and looked respectfully toward the Worship-object on the stage. The guardians nodded approvingly. Apparently it had been the right gesture. She relaxed a bit, waiting, wondering what would happen next.

The door guard responded to a second knock and announced a second entry. "The accuser, Vandara!" he called.

So: it was to be the two of them. Kira watched as Vandara strode rapidly toward the table until they were side by side, facing the Council of Guardians. It gave her a small feeling of satisfaction to notice that Vandara's feet were bare and her face dirty; the woman had made no special preparations. Perhaps none was necessary. But Kira felt that possibly she had gained a small bit of respect, a small advantage, with her cleanliness.

Vandara made the worshipful gesture with her hands. So they were even there. Then Vandara bowed, and Kira saw with a twinge of concern that the Guardians nodded their heads toward her.

I should have bowed. I must find an occasion to bow.

"We meet to pass judgment on a conflict." The chief guardian, a white-haired man with a four-syllable name that Kira could never remember, spoke in an authoritative voice.

I had no conflict. I only wanted to rebuild my cott and live my life.

"Who is the accuser?" the white-haired man asked. Of course he knew the answer, Kira thought. But the question seemed to be ceremonial, part of the formal proceedings. It was answered by another of the guardians, a heavy-set man at the end of the table who had several thick books and a stack of papers in front of him. Kira eyed the volumes curiously. She had always yearned to read. But women were not allowed.

"Chief guardian, the accuser is the woman Vandara."

"And the accused?"

"The accused is the orphan girl Kira." The man glanced at the papers but didn't seem to be reading anything.

Accused? What am I accused of? Hearing the repetition of the word, Kira felt a wave of panic. *But I
can use it as a chance to bow and show humility.* She
inclined her head and upper body slightly, acknowl-
edging herself as the accused.

The white-haired man looked at the two of them
dispassionately. Kira, leaning on her stick, tried to
stand as straight as possible. She was almost as tall as
her accuser. But Vandara was older, heavier, and
unflawed except for the scar, the reminder that she
had fought a beast and escaped alive. Hideous
though it was, the scar emphasized her strength.
Kira's flaw carried no illustrious history, and she felt
weak, inadequate, and doomed beside the disfigured,
angry woman.

"The accuser will speak first," the chief guardian
instructed.

Vandara's voice was firm and bitter. "The girl
should have been taken to the Field when she was
born and still nameless. It is the way."

"Go on," the chief guardian said.

"She was imperfect. And fatherless as well. She
should not have been kept."

*But I was strong. And my eyes were bright. My
mother told me. She wouldn't let me go.* Kira shifted
her weight, resting her twisted leg, remembering the
story of her birth, and wondering if she would have
an opportunity to tell it here. *I gripped her thumb so
tightly.*

"We have all tolerated her presence for these

26

years," Vandara went on. "But she has not contributed. She cannot dig or plant or weed, or even tend the domestic beasts the way other girls her age do. She drags that dead leg around like a useless burden. She is slow, and she eats a lot."

The Council of Guardians was listening carefully. Kira's face felt warm with embarrassment. It was true, that she ate a lot. It was *all* true, what her accuser was saying.

I can try to eat less. I can go hungry. In her mind, Kira prepared her defense, but even as she did, she felt that it would be weak and whining.

"She was kept, against the rules, because her grandfather was still alive and had power. But he is long gone, replaced by a new leader with *more* power and wisdom —"

Vandara oozed compliments designed to strengthen her case, and Kira glanced at the chief guardian to see if he was swayed by the flattery. But his face was impassive.

"Her father was killed by beasts even before her birth. And now her mother is dead," Vandara went on. "There is even reason to think that her mother may have carried an illness that will endanger others —"

No! She was the only one to fall ill! Look at me! I lay beside her when she died, and I am not ill!

"— and the women need the space where their cott was. There is no room for this useless girl. She can't marry. No one wants a cripple. She takes up

27

space, and food, and she causes problems with the discipline of the tykes, telling them stories, teaching them games so that they make noise and disrupt the work —"

The chief guardian waved his hand. "Enough," he announced.

Vandara frowned and fell silent. She bowed slightly.

The chief guardian looked around the table at the eleven others as if he sought comments or questions. One by one they nodded at him. No one said anything.

"Kira," the white-haired chief guardian said, "as a two-syllable girl, you are not required to defend yourself."

"Not defend myself? But —" Kira had planned to bow again, but forgot in her urgency. Now she remembered, but her bow was an awkward afterthought.

He waved his hand again, signaling her silence. She forced herself to be still and to listen.

"Because of your youth," he explained, "you have a choice. You may defend yourself —"

She interrupted again, unable to stop. "Oh, yes! I want to def —"

He ignored her outburst. "Or we will appoint a defender on your behalf. One of us will defend you, using our greater wisdom and experience. Take a moment to think about this, because your life may depend upon it, Kira."

But you are strangers to me! How can you tell the story of my birth? How can you describe my bright eyes, the strength of my hand as I gripped my mother's thumb?

Kira stood helplessly, her future at stake. She felt the hostility beside her; Vandara's breath was quick and angry though her voice had been silenced. She looked at the men seated around the table, trying to assess them as defenders. But she felt from them neither hostility nor much interest, just a sense of expectation as they waited for her decision.

As Kira agonized, her hands pushed their way into the deep pockets of her woven shift. She felt the familiar outline of her mother's wooden comb and stroked it for comfort. With her thumb she felt a small square of decorated woven cloth. She had forgotten the strip of cloth in the recent confusing days; now she remembered how this one, this design, had come, unbidden to her hands as she sat beside her mother in the last days.

When she was much younger, the knowledge had come quite unexpectedly to her, and she recalled the look of amazement on her mother's face as she watched Kira choose and pattern the threads one afternoon with a sudden sureness. "I didn't teach you that!" her mother said, laughing with delight and astonishment. "I wouldn't know how!" Kira hadn't known how either, not really. It had come about almost magically, as if the threads had spoken to her, or sung. After that first time, the knowledge had grown.

She clutched the cloth, remembering the sense of certainty it had given to her. She felt none of that sureness now. A speech of defense was not within her. She knew she would have to relinquish that role to one of these men, all strangers.

She looked at them with frightened eyes and saw one looking calmly, reassuringly back. She sensed his importance to her. She sensed something more: awareness, experience. Kira took a deep breath. The threaded cloth was warm and familiar in her hand. She trembled. But her voice was certain. "Please appoint a defender," she said.

The chief guardian nodded. "Jamison," he said firmly and nodded to the third man on his left.

The man with the calm, attentive eyes rose to defend Kira. She waited.

4

So that was his name: Jamison. It was not familiar to her. There were so many in the village, and the separation of male and female was so great, after childhood had ended.

Kira watched him stand. He was tall, with longish dark hair neatly combed and clasped at the back of his neck with a carved wooden ornament that she recognized as the work of the young woodcarver — what was his name? Thomas. That was it. Thomas the Carver, they called him. He was still a boy, no older than Kira herself, but already he had been singled out for his great gifts, and the carvings that came from his skilled hands were much in demand among the elite of the village. Ordinary people did not ornament themselves. Kira's mother had worn a pendant hanging from a thong around her neck but she kept it hidden, always, inside the neck of her dress.

Her defender picked up the stack of papers on the table before him; Kira had watched him marking these papers meticulously as he listened to the accuser. His hands were large, long-fingered, and sure in their movements; no hesitancy, no uncertainty. She

31

saw that he wore a bracelet of braided leather on his right wrist, and that his arm, bare above the bracelet, was sinewy and muscular. He was not old. His name, Jamison, was still three syllables, and his hair had not grayed. She judged him to be midlife, perhaps the same age that her mother had been.

He looked down at the top paper of the stack in his hands. From where she stood, Kira could see the markings that he was examining. How she wished she could read!

Then he spoke. "I will address the accusations one by one," he said. Looking at the paper, he repeated the words that Vandara had said, though he did not imitate her rage-laden tone. "The girl should have been taken to the Field when she was born and still nameless. It is the way.'"

So that was what he had marked! He had written the words so that he could repeat them! Painful though it was to hear the accusations repeated, Kira realized with awe the value of the repetition. There would be no argument, afterward, about what had been said. How often among the tykes fistfights and battles had begun from You said, I said, He said that you said, and the infinite variations.

Jamison set the papers on the table and picked up a heavy volume bound in green leather. Kira noticed that each of the guardians had an identical volume.

He opened to a page he had marked during the proceedings. Kira had seen him turning the pages of the volume as Vandara had made her accusatory presentation.

"The accuser is correct that it is the way," Jamison said to the guardians. Kira felt stricken by the betrayal. Hadn't he been appointed her defender?

He was pointing now to a page, to its densely written text. Kira saw some of the men turn in their green volumes, finding the same passage. Others simply nodded, as if they remembered it so clearly there was no need to reread.

She saw Vandara smile slightly.

Defeated, Kira felt again the small cloth square in her pocket. Its warmth was gone. Its comfort was gone.

"Turning, though," Jamison was saying, "to the third set of amendments —"

The guardians all turned pages in their books. Even those whose volumes had remained closed now picked them up and looked for the place.

"It is clear that exceptions can be made."

"Exceptions can be made," one of the guardians repeated, reading the words, his fingers moving on the page.

"So we may set aside the assertion that it is the way," Jamison announced with certainty. "It need not *always* be the way."

He is my defender. Perhaps he will find a way to let me live!

"Do you wish to speak?" the defender asked Kira.

Touching her scrap of cloth, she shook her

head no.

He went on, consulting his notes. "She was imperfect. And fatherless as well. She should not have been kept." The second repetition hurt, because it was true. Kira's leg hurt too. She was not accustomed to standing so still for so long. She tried to shift her weight to ease the pressure on her flawed side.

"These accusations are true." Jamison repeated the obvious, in his steady voice. "The girl Kira was imperfect at birth. She had a visible and incurable defect."

The guardians were staring at her. So was Vandara, with contempt. Kira was accustomed to stares. She had been taunted throughout her childhood. With her mother as teacher and guide, she had learned to hold her head high. She did so now, looking her judges in the eyes.

"And fatherless as well," Jamison continued.

In her memory, Kira could hear her mother's voice explaining it to her. She was small then, and wondering why she had never had a father. "He did not return from the great hunt. It was before you were born," her mother said gently. "He was taken by beasts."

She heard Jamison repeat the words of her thoughts as if they had been audible. "Before her birth, her father was taken by beasts," Jamison explained.

The chief guardian looked up from his papers.

Turning to the others at the table, he interrupted Jamison. "Her father was Christopher. He was a fine hunter, one of the best. Some of you probably remember him."

Several of the men nodded. Her defender nodded as well. "I was with the hunting party that day," he said. "I saw him taken."

You saw my father taken? Kira had never heard the details of the tragedy. She knew only what her mother had told her. But this man had known her father. This man had been there!

Was he afraid? Was my father afraid? It was a strange, unbiddden question, and she did not ask it aloud. But Kira was so afraid herself. She could feel Vandara's hatred as a presence by her side. She felt as if she were being taken by beasts; as if she were about to die. She wondered what the moment had been like for her father.

"The third amendment applies here, as well," Jamison announced. "To the accusation 'She should not have been kept,' I reply that according to the third amendment, exceptions may be made."

The chief guardian nodded. "Her father was a fine hunter," he said again. The others at the table, taking their lead from him, murmured in agreement.

"Do you wish to speak?" they asked her. Again she shook her head. Again she felt, for the moment, spared.

"'But she has not contributed,'" Jamison read next. "'She cannot dig or plant or weed, or even tend the domestic beasts the way other girls her age do. She drags that dead leg around like a useless burden. She is slow,'" he continued, and then Kira saw a hint of a smile as he concluded, "'and she eats a lot.'"

The man stood silent for a moment. Then he said, "As defender, I am going to concede some of these points. It is clear that she cannot dig or plant or weed or tend domestic beasts. I believe, however, that she has found a way to contribute. Am I correct, Kira, that you work at the weaving shed?"

Kira nodded, surprised. How did he know? Men paid no attention to the work of women.

"Yes," she said, her voice soft from nervousness. "I help there. Not with the actual weaving. But I clean up the scraps and help prepare the looms. It is work I can do with my hands and arms. And I am strong."

She wondered if she should mention her skill with the threads, her hope that perhaps she could use it as a way of making a living. But she couldn't think of a way to say it without sounding vain, so she kept still.

"Kira," he said, looking toward her, "demonstrate your flaw for the Council of Guardians. Let us see you walk. Go to the door and back."

It was cruel of him, she thought. They all knew about her twisted leg. Why did she have to do this in front of them, to submit to their humiliating stares? For a moment she was tempted to refuse, or at least to argue. But the stakes were too high. This was not a tykes' game, where arguing and fighting were expected. This was what would determine her future, or whether she had a future. Kira sighed and turned. She leaned on her stick and walked slowly to the door. Biting her lip, she dragged her aching leg step by step, and felt Vandara's contemptuous eyes on her back.

At the door Kira turned and came slowly back to her place. Pain started in her foot and seared through her twisted leg. She longed to sit.

"She does drag her leg, and she is slow," Jamison pointed out needlessly. "I concede those points.

"Yet her work at the weaving shed is competent. She goes each day for regular hours, and she is never late. The women there value her help.

"Does she eat a lot?" he asked, and chuckled. "I think not. Look how thin she is. Her weight refutes that accusation.

"But I suspect she is hungry now," he said. "I am. I suggest we take a break for a meal."

The chief guardian stood. "Do you wish to speak?" he asked Kira for the third time. For the third time she shook her head no. She felt terribly tired.

"You may sit," he directed Kira and Vandara. "Food will be brought."

Gratefully Kira lowered herself onto the nearby bench. She rubbed her throbbing leg with one hand. Across the aisle, she saw Vandara bow — *I forgot again! I should have bowed!* — and then sit, stony-faced.

The chief guardian glanced down at his own stack of papers. "There are five more charges," he said. "We will deal with them and make a decision after the meal."

Food appeared, brought by the door guard. A plate was handed to Kira. She saw and smelled roasted chicken and warm, crusty bread scattered with seeds. She had not eaten anything but raw vegetables in several days, and had not tasted chicken in many months. But she could still hear Vandara's voice, shrill with vindictive accusation: "She eats a lot."

Fearful of the consequences if she showed her ravenous hunger, Kira willed herself to nibble at the tempting meal. Then she set the half-empty plate aside and sipped water from the cup they had brought. Tired, hungry still, and frightened, she stroked the scrap of cloth in her pocket, and waited for the next round of accusations.

The twelve guardians went elsewhere, leaving through a side door, probably to a private eating place. After a while guards came to take her food tray away and announced a rest period. The trial would resume when the bell rang twice, they told her. Vandara rose and left the room. Kira waited for a moment. Then she made her way to the door of the Council Edifice, walked through the long hall, and went outside.

The world was unchanged. People came and went, working at various jobs, arguing loudly. She heard shrill voices at the marketplace: women shouting outrage at the prices, vendors shouting in reply. Babies cried, tykes fought, scavenger dogs growled and menaced each other as they vied for dropped scraps.

The boy Matt appeared, running past with some others. When he saw Kira he hesitated, then stopped and came back.

"We got saplings for you," he whispered. "Me and some other tykes. We put 'em in a pile. Later we be starting your cott if you want." Then he paused, curious. "If you need a cott, that is. What be happening in there?"

So Matt knew about the trial. No surprise. The boy seemed to know everything that was happening in the village. Kira shrugged with feigned nonchalance. She didn't want to let him know how frightened she was. "A lot of talking," she told the boy.

"And she be in there? Her with the horrid scar?"

Kira knew whom he meant. "Yes. She's the accuser."

"She's hard, that Vandara. She killed her own tyke, they say. Made him eat the oleander, they say. Sat with him and held his head till he et it, though he didn't want to."

Kira had heard the story. "It was judged an accident," she reminded Matt, though she had her doubts. "Other tykes have eaten the oleander. It's a danger, having a poisonous plant grow wild everywhere. They ought to pull it all up, not leave it where the tykes can get at it."

Matt shook his head. "We be needing it there to teach us," he pointed out. "Me mum, she slapped at me when I touched it. Slapped my head around so horrid hard I thought my neck would crack. It's how I learnt about the oleander."

"Well, the Council of Guardians judged Vandara and said she didn't," Kira said again.

"She's a hard one, anyways. They say because of the horrid wound. Pain be making her cruel."

Pain made me proud, Kira thought but didn't say.

"When you be finish?"

"Later today."

"We'll work on your cott. Some of my mates'll help."

"Thank you, Matt," Kira said. "You're a good friend."

He made a face, embarrassed. "You be needing a cott." He turned to run after the other boys. "And you tell us the stories, after all. You be needing a place for that."

Kira smiled, watching him scamper off. The bell at the top of the Council Edifice rang twice. She turned to reenter the building.

"'She was kept, against the rules, because her grandfather was still alive and had power. But he is long gone.'"

Jamison read the next accusation on the list.

They had allowed her to sit for the afternoon session. And they told Vandara to sit too. Kira was grateful. If Vandara had stood, she would have forced herself to ignore the pain in her leg and stand as well.

Again the guardian who was her defender reiterated that exceptions could be made. By now, frightening though the accusations were, the repetition was tiresome. Kira tried to stay alert. With her hand in her pocket, she fingered the small scrap of woven cloth and pictured its colors in her mind.

The community cloth was drab, all no-color; the formless shifts and trousers worn by the people were woven and stitched for protection against the sudden occasional rain, thorn scratch, or poison berry. The usual village fabric was not decorated.

But Kira's mother had known the art of dye. It was from her stained hands that the colored threads used for rare ornamentation were produced. The robe worn each year by the Singer when he performed the Ruin Song was richly embroidered. The intricate scenes on it had been there for centuries, and the robe had been worn by each Singer and passed from one to the next. Once, many years before, Katrina had been asked to replace a few threads that had torn loose. Kira was only a small tyke then, but she remembered standing in the cott's shadowed corner when a guardian brought the fabulous robe and waited while her mother made the small repair. She remembered watching, fascinated, as her mother pushed a bone needle with thick colorful thread through the fabric; gradually a bright gold replaced the small frayed spot on one sleeve. Then they had taken the robe away again.

At that year's Gathering, Kira remembered, both she and her mother had peered from their seats at the stage, trying to find the repaired place as the Singer moved his arms in gestures during the Song. But they were too far away, and the repaired spot was too small.

Each year that followed, they had brought the ancient robe again to her mother for small repairs.

"One day my daughter will be able to do this," Katrina had said one year to the guardian. "Look what she has done!" she said and showed him the scrap that Kira had just completed, the one that had composed itself so magically in her fingers. "She has a skill far greater than mine."

Kira had stood silently, embarrassed but proud, as the guardian examined the threading she had done. He made no comment, simply nodded and returned the small piece to her. But his eyes had been bright with interest, she could see. Each year following, he had asked to see her work.

Kira always stood at her mother's side, never touching the fragile ancient cloth, marveling each time at the rich hues that told the history of the world. Golds and reds and browns. And here and there, faded pale, almost reduced to white, there had once been blue. Her mother showed her the faded places that remained of it.

Her mother did not know how to make blue. Sometimes they talked of it, Kira and Katrina, looking at the huge upturned bowl of sky above their world. "If only I could make blue," her mother said. "I've heard that somewhere there is a special plant." She looked out at her own garden, thick with the flowers and shoots from which she could create the golds and greens and pinks, and shook her head in yearning for the one color she could not create.

Now her mother was dead.

Now her mother is dead.

Kira startled herself out of the daydreamed memory. Someone was saying those words. She made herself listen.

"'— and now her mother is dead. There is even reason to think that her mother may have carried an illness that will endanger others —

"'— and the women need the space where their cott was. There is no room for this useless girl. She can't marry. No one wants a cripple. She takes up space, and food, and she causes problems with the discipline of the tykes, telling them stories, teaching them games so that they make noise and disrupt the work.'"

It dragged on. The repetitions of Vandara's accusations were recited, and the defender again and again reiterated the amendment that said exceptions could be made.

But Kira noted a change of tone. It was subtle, but she perceived a difference. Something had taken place among the Council of Guardians when the members had withdrawn during lunch. She saw Vandara shift uneasily in her seat and knew that her accuser noticed the difference too.

Kira, clutching the cloth talisman in her pocket, became aware suddenly that its warmth and comfort had returned.

During her infrequent leisure times, Kira often experimented with colored bits of threadings, feeling the excitement in her fingers as her surprising skill grew. She used bits of discarded woven cloth from the weaving shed. It was not a violation. She had asked permission to take the scraps to her cott.

Sometimes, pleased with what she had done, she showed her work to her mother and received a proud, quick smile of approval. But more often her efforts were disappointments, the uneven products of a girl still learning; usually she threw her experiments away.

This one, the one she held now in the nervous fingers of her right hand, she had done as her mother lay ill. Seated helplessly by the side of the dying woman, Kira leaned forward again and again to hold a container of water to her mother's lips. She smoothed her mother's hair, rubbed her cold feet, and held the trembling hands, knowing there was nothing more she could do. While her mother slept restlessly, Kira sorted the dyed threads in her basket and began to weave them into the cloth scrap with a bone needle. It soothed her to do so, and passed the time.

The threads began to sing to her. Not a song of words or tones, but a pulsing, a quivering in her hands as if they had life. For the first time, her fingers did not direct the threads, but followed where they led. She was able to close her eyes and simply feel the needle move through the fabric, pulled by the urgent, vibrating threads.

When her mother murmured, Kira leaned forward with the water container and moistened the dry lips. Only then did she look down at the small strip of material in her lap. It was radiant. Despite the dim light in the cott — it was night-start by then — the golds and reds pulsated as if the morning sun itself had slid and twisted its rays into the cloth. The brilliant threads crisscrossed in an intricate pattern of loops and knots that Kira had never seen before, that she could not have created, that she had never known or heard described.

When her mother's eyes opened for a final time, Kira had held the vibrant piece of fabric so that the dying woman could see. Words were beyond Katrina by then. But she smiled.

Now, secret in her hand, the cloth seemed to speak a silent, pulsing message to Kira. It told her there was danger still. But it told her also that she was to be saved.

5

Kira noticed for the first time that a large box had been placed on the floor behind the seats of the Council of Guardians.

It had not been there before the lunchtime break.

As she and Vandara watched, one of the guards, responding to a nod from the chief guardian, lifted the box to the table and raised its lid. Her defender, Jamison, removed and unfolded something that she recognized immediately.

"The Singer's robe!" Kira spoke aloud in delight.

"This has no relevance," Vandara muttered. But she too was leaning forward to see.

The magnificent robe was laid out on the table in display. Ordinarily it was seen only once a year, at the time when the village gathered to hear the Ruin Song, the lengthy history of their people. Most citizens, crowded into the auditorium for the occasion, saw the Singer's robe only from a distance; they shoved and pushed, trying to nudge closer for a look.

But Kira knew the robe well from watching her mother's meticulous work on it each year. A guardian had always stood nearby, attentive. Warned not to touch, Kira had watched, marveling at her mother's skill, at her ability to choose just the right shade.

There, on the left shoulder! Kira remembered that spot, where just last year some threads had pulled and torn and her mother had carefully coaxed the broken threads free. Then she had selected pale pinks, slightly darker roses, and other colors darkening to crimson, each hue only a hint deeper than the one before; and she had stitched them into place, blending them flawlessly into the edges of the elaborate design.

Jamison watched Kira as she remembered. Then he said, "Your mother had been teaching you the art."

Kira nodded. "Since I was small," she acknowledged aloud.

"Your mother was a skilled worker. Her dyes were steadfast. They have not faded."

"She was careful," Kira said, "and thorough."

"We are told that your skill is greater than hers."

So they knew. "I still have much to learn," Kira said.

"And she taught you the coloring, as well as the stitches?"

Kira nodded because she knew he expected her to. But it was not exactly true. Her mother had planned to teach her the art of the dyes, but the time had not yet come before the illness struck. She tried to be honest in her answer. "She was beginning to teach me," Kira said. "She told me that she had been taught by a woman named Annabel."

"Annabella now," Jamison said.

Kira was startled. "She is still alive? And four syllables?"

"She is very old. Her sight is somewhat diminished. But she can still be used as a resource."

Resource for what? But Kira stayed silent. The scrap in her pocket was warm against her hand.

Suddenly Vandara stood. "I request that these proceedings continue," she said abruptly and harshly. "This is a delaying tactic on the part of the defender."

The chief guardian rose. Around him, the other guardians, who had been murmuring among themselves, fell silent.

His voice, directed at Vandara, was not unkind. "You may go," he said. "The proceedings are complete. We have reached our decision."

Vandara stood silent, unmoving. She glared at him defiantly. The chief guardian nodded, and two guards moved forward to escort her from the room.

"I have a right to know your decision!" Vandara shouted, her face twisted with rage. She wrested her arms free of the guards' grasp and faced the Council of Guardians.

"Actually," the chief guardian said in a calm voice, "you have no rights at all. But I am going to tell you the decision so that there will be no misunderstanding.

"The orphan girl Kira will stay. She will have a

new role."

He gestured toward the Singer's robe, still spread out on the table. "Kira," he said, looking at her, "you will continue your mother's work. You will go beyond her work, actually, since your skill is far greater than hers was. First, you will repair the robe, as your mother always did. Next, you will restore it. Then your true work will begin. You will *complete* the robe." He gestured toward the large undecorated expanse of fabric across the shoulders. He raised one eyebrow, looking at her as if he were asking a question.

Nervously Kira nodded in reply and bowed slightly.

"As for you?" The chief guardian looked again at Vandara, who stood sullenly between the guards. He spoke politely to her. "You have not lost. You demanded the girl's land, and you may have it, you and the other women. Build your pen. It would be wise to pen your tykes; they are troublesome and should be better contained.

"Go now," he commanded.

Vandara turned. Her face was a mask of fury. She shrugged away the hands of the guards, leaned forward, and whispered harshly to Kira, "You will fail. Then they will kill you."

She smiled coldly at Jamison. "So, that's it, then," she said. "The girl is yours." She stalked down the aisle and went through the broad door.

The chief guardian and the other Council members ignored the outburst, as if it were merely an annoying insect that had finally been swatted away. Someone was refolding the Singer's robe.

"Kira," Jamison said, "go and gather what you need. Whatever you want to bring with you. Be back here when the bell rings four times. And we will take you to your quarters, to the place where you will live from now on."

Puzzled, Kira waited a moment. But there were no other instructions. The guardians were straightening their papers and collecting their books and belongings. They seemed to have forgotten she was there. Finally she stood, straightened herself against her walking stick, and limped from the room.

Emerging from the Council Edifice into bright sunlight and the usual chaos of the village central plaza, she realized that it was still midafternoon, still an ordinary day in the existence of the people, and that no one's life had changed except her own.

The summer-start day was hot. Near the Edifice steps, a crowd had gathered to watch a pig-slaughter behind the butcher's. After the choice parts were sold, scraps would be thrown. People and dogs together would shove and grab. The smell from the thick mounds of excrement beneath the terrified pigs and the high-pitched squeals of terror as they awaited death made Kira feel dizzy and nauseated. She hurried around the edge of the throng, making her way toward the weaving shed.

"You're out! What happened? Do you go to the Field? To the beasts?"

Matt was calling to her in excitement. Kira smiled. His curiosity appealed to her — it matched her own — and behind his wildness he had a kind heart, she thought. She remembered how he had acquired his pet, his little companion dog. It had been a useless stray, underfoot, scavenging everywhere for food. On a rainy afternoon it had been caught and tossed by the wheel of a passing donkey cart. Badly injured, the dog lay bleeding in the mud and would have been left to die unnoticed. But the boy hid it in nearby shrubbery until its wounds had mended. Kira had watched from the weaving shed each day as Matt stealthily crept in to feed the animal while it lay healing. Now the dog, lively and in good health despite a tail as crooked and useless as Kira's leg, stayed constantly at Matt's side. He called it Branch, named for the small tree part he had used to splint its damaged tail.

Kira reached down and scratched the homely mongrel behind his ear. "I'm let go," she told the boy.

His eyes widened. Then he grinned. "So we still be getting stories, me and my mates," he said with satisfaction.

"I seen Vandara," Matt added. "She come out like this." He scampered to the steps of the Edifice and stalked down them, face haughty. Kira smiled at the imitation.

"She be hating you now for certain," Matt

51

added cheerfully.

"Well, they gave her my piece of land," Kira told him, "so she and the others can make a pen for their tykes, the way they wanted.

"I hope you didn't already start on a new cott for me," she added, remembering that he had offered.

Matt grinned. "We didn't start yet," he said. "Soon we would've. But if you be sent to the beasts, then there be no need."

He paused, rubbing Branch with his dirty bare foot. "Where you to live, then?"

Kira slapped at a mosquito on her arm. She rubbed at the little smear of blood from its bite. "I don't know," she admitted. "They told me to come back to the Edifice when the bell rings four. I'm to gather my things." She laughed a little. "I don't have much to gather. My things were mostly burned."

Matt grinned. "I saved you some things," he told her happily. "I filched 'em from your cott before the burning. Didn't tell you before. I waited to see what be happening to you."

Down the path, beyond the pig-slaughter, Matt's mates called to him to hurry and join them. "Me and Branch must go along now," he said, "but I be bringing the things to you when the bells go four. To the steps, aye?"

"Thank you, Matt. I'll meet you at the steps." Smiling, Kira watched him go, his thin, scabbed legs churning in the dusty path as he ran to join his friends. Beside him, Branch scampered, his broken stub of a tail wagging crookedly.

Kira continued on through the crowds, past the food shops and the noise of bickering, bargaining women. Dogs barked; a pair of them snarled, facing each other with bared teeth in the path, a dropped morsel between them. Nearby, a curly-headed tyke eyed both dogs warily then deftly leaped between them, seized the bit of food, and stuffed it into his own mouth. His mother, intent on her business at a nearby shop, glanced around, saw the tyke near the dogs, and seized him away, yanking at his arm and administering a sharp slap to his head when he was back at her side. The tyke smirked, chewing eagerly at whatever he had picked up from the path.

The weaving shed was farther along, mercifully in a shady area surrounded by large trees. It was quieter there and cooler, though the mosquitoes were more numerous. The women in the shed, seated at looms, nodded to Kira as she approached. "There's plenty scraps to gather," one called and gestured with her head as her hands continued work.

It was the job that Kira usually did, the tidying up. She was not permitted to weave yet, though she had always watched carefully how it was done and thought that she could have, if they needed her.

She had not been at the weaving shed in many days, not since her mother's illness and death. So much had happened. So much had changed. She assumed that she would not be returning now that her status seemed different. But because they had called to her in a friendly way, Kira moved through the shed, through the clatter of the wooden looms at work, and picked up the scraps from the floor. One loom was silent, she noticed. No one was working there today. Fourth from the end, she counted. Usually Camilla was there.

She paused by the empty loom and waited until a nearby worker had stopped to reset her shuttle.

"Where is Camilla?" Kira asked curiously. Sometimes, of course, the women left briefly, to wed, to give birth, or simply assigned to some other temporary task.

The weaver glanced over, her hands still occupied. Her feet began to move again on the treadle. "She fell, took a clumsy fall, over at the stream." She gestured with her head. "Doing washing. The rocks were mossy."

"Yes, it's slippery there." Kira knew. She had slipped herself sometimes at the stream, at the washing place.

The woman shrugged. "She broke her arm real bad. Can't be fixed. Can't be made straight. No more good for weaving. Her hubby tried real hard to straighten up the arm 'cause he needs her. For the tykes and such. But she'll probably go to the Field."

Kira shuddered, imagining the torturing pain of the broken arm as the hubby tried to pull it into a healing shape.

"She has five tykes, Camilla does. Now she can't care for them, or work. They'll be given away. You want one?" The woman grinned at Kira. She had few teeth.

Kira shook her head. She smiled wanly and continued down the aisle between the looms.

"You want her loom?" the woman called after her. "They'll be needing somebody to take it. You're probably ready to weave."

But Kira shook her head again. She had wanted to weave, once. The weaving women had always been kind to her. But her future seemed different now.

The looms clattered on. From the shade of the shed, Kira noticed that the sun was lower in the sky. It would soon be the ringing of four bells. She nodded goodbye to the weaving women and headed back along the path toward the place where she had lived with her mother, the place where her cott had long stood, the place of the only home she had ever known. She felt a need to say goodbye.

6

The huge bell in the tower of the Council Edifice began to ring. The bell governed the people's lives. It told them when to begin work and when to stop, when to gather for meetings, when to prepare for a hunt, celebrate an event, or arm for danger. Four bells — the third was resonating now — meant that the day's business could end. For Kira, it meant the time to report to the Council of Guardians. She hurried toward the central plaza through the crowds of people leaving their workplaces.

Matt was waiting on the steps as he had promised. Branch, beside him, was pawing excitedly at a large iridescent beetle, blocking its path again and again with a paw as the beetle tried unsuccessfully to waddle by. The dog looked up and wagged its crooked tail when Kira called a greeting.

"What you got?" Matt asked, looking at the small bundle Kira carried on her back.

"Not much." She laughed ruefully. "But I had stored a few things in the clearing so they missed the burning. My basket of threads, and some scraps of cloth. And look at this, Matt." She reached into her pocket and held up a lumpy oblong. "I found my soap where I left it on a rock. Good thing, because I don't know how to make it, and I have no coins to buy any."

Then she laughed, realizing that Matt, grimy and unkempt, felt no need of soap. She supposed Matt had a mother somewhere, and usually mothers scrubbed their tykes now and then, but she had never known Matt clean.

"Here, I brung these." Matt indicated a pile of objects wrapped haphazardly in a dirty woven cloth on the step near him. "Some things I took before the burning, for you to have iffen they let you stay."

"Thank you, Matt." Kira wondered what he had chosen to rescue.

"But you'll not be carrying it because of your horrid gimp," he said, referring to her crippled leg. "So I'll be your carrier, once they tells you where you're to be. That way I'll know too."

Kira liked the idea of Matt coming with her and knowing where she would live. It made everything seem less strange. "Wait here, then," she told him. "I must go inside, and they'll show me where I'll be living. Then I'll come back for you. I have to hurry, Matt, because the bells have finished, and they told me to come at four bells."

"Me and Branch can wait. I've got me a sucker I filched from a shop," Matt said, pulling a dirt-encrusted candy from his pocket, "and Branch, him always loves a mammoth buggie to poke, like now."

57

The dog's ears shot up at the sound of his name but his eyes never left the beetle on the step.

Kira hurried inside the Council Edifice while the boy waited on the steps.

Only Jamison was in the large room waiting for her. She wondered if having been appointed her defender at the trial, he was now to be her overseer. Oddly she felt a little twinge of irritation. She was old enough to manage alone. Many girls her age were preparing for marriage. She had always known she would not marry — her twisted leg made it an impossibility; she could never be a good wife, could never perform the many duties required — but certainly she could manage alone. Her mother had, and had taught her.

But he nodded in welcome and her brief irritation faded and was forgotten.

"There you are," Jamison said. He rose and folded the papers he'd been reading. "I'll show you to your quarters. It isn't far. It's in a wing of this building."

Then he looked at her and at the small bundle she carried on her back. "Is that all you have?" he asked.

She was glad that he had inquired because it gave her the opportunity to mention Matt.

"Not quite," Kira told him. "But I can't carry much because of —" She gestured toward her leg. Jamison nodded.

"So I have a boy who helps me. His name is Matt. I hope you don't mind, but he's waiting on the steps.

He has my other things. I was hoping that maybe you would let him continue as my helper. He's a good boy."

Jamison frowned slightly. Then he turned and called to one of the guards. "Get the boy from the steps," he said.

"Ah," Kira interrupted. Both Jamison and the guard turned. She felt awkward and spoke apologetically. She even felt herself bow slightly. "He has a dog," she said in a low voice. "He won't go anyplace without his dog.

"It's quite small," she added in a whisper.

Jamison looked at her impatiently, as if he were suddenly aware what a burden she was going to be. Finally he sighed. "Bring the dog too," he told the guard.

The three of them were led down a corridor. They were an odd trio, with Kira first, stumbling against her stick, dragging her leg with its broom sound: swish, swish; then Matt, silent for a change, his eyes wide, taking in the grandeur of the surroundings; and finally, toenails tip-tapping against the tiled floor, the bent-tailed dog, happily carrying a squirming beetle in his mouth.

Matt put the bundle of Kira's belongings down on the floor just inside the doorway, but he wouldn't step inside the room. He took in everything solemnly with his wide-eyed, observant gaze and made the decision himself.

"Me and Branch, we'll wait out here," he announced. "What this be called?" he asked, looking around the wide space where he stood.

"The corridor," Jamison told him.

Matt nodded. "Me and Branch, we just be waiting here in this corridor then. Me and Branch, we don't go in the room because of the wee buggies."

Kira looked over quickly, but the beetle had been consumed now. Anyway, the beetle had not been wee. Matt himself had described it as mammoth.

"Wee buggies?" Jamison was the one who inquired, his brow furrowed.

"Branch got fleas," Matt explained, looking at the floor.

Jamison shook his head. Kira saw his lips twitch in amusement. He led her into the room.

She was astonished. The cott where she had lived all of her life with her mother had been a simple dirt-floored hut. Their beds had been straw-filled pallets on raised wooden shelves. Handmade utensils had held their belongings and food; they had always eaten together at a wooden table that Kira's father had made long before her birth. She mourned the table after the burning because of the memories it held for her mother. Katrina had described his strong hands smoothing the wood and rounding its corners so that the coming baby would not be endangered by sharp edges. All of it was ashes now: the smooth wood, the soft edges, the memory of his hands.

This room had several tables, skillfully made, carved and delicate. And the bed was wood, on legs, covered with lightly woven bed coverings. Kira had never seen such a bed and supposed the raised legs were to make one safe from beasts or bugs. Yet surely there were none here, in the Council Edifice; even Matt had sensed that and consigned his dog's fleas to the corridor. There were windows, with glass, and through them she could see the tops of trees; the room faced the forest behind the building.

Jamison opened a door inside the room, and Kira saw a smaller room, windowless, lined with wide drawers.

"The Singer's robe is kept here," he told her. He opened one large drawer slightly and she saw the folded robe with its bright threaded colors. He closed it again and gestured toward the other, smaller drawers.

"Supplies," he said. "Whatever you need."

He moved back into the bedroom and opened a door on the other side. She caught a glimpse of what at first seemed flat stones; it was a floor of pale green tile. "There is water here," he explained, "for washing and all your needs."

Water? Inside a building?

Jamison went to the doorway and glanced out to where Matt and Branch waited. Matt was squatting on the floor and sucking on his stick of candy.

"If you want the boy to stay with you, you could wash him here. The dog too. There is a tub."

61

Matt heard him and looked up toward Kira in dismay. "No. Me and Branch, we be going now," he said. Then with an expression of concern, he asked, "You don't be captive here, do you?"

"No, she's not a captive," Jamison reassured Matt. "Why would you think that?

"Your supper will be brought," he told Kira. "You're not alone here. The Carver lives down the hall, on the other side." He gestured with his hand to a closed door.

"The Carver? Do you mean the boy named Thomas?" Kira was startled. "He lives here too?"

"Yes. You are welcome to visit his room. You must both work during the daylight hours, but you may take your meals with the Carver. Familiarize yourself with your quarters now, and your tools. Get some rest. Tomorrow I will go over your work assignment with you.

"I'll lead the boy and the dog out now."

She stood in the open doorway and watched them retreat down the long corridor, the man leading the way, Matt walking jauntily just behind him, and the dog at Matt's heels. The boy looked back at her, waved slightly, and grinned with a questioning look. His face, smeared with the sticky candy, was alight with excitement. She knew that within minutes he would be telling his mates that he'd barely escaped being washed. His dog too, and all the fleas; a close call.

Quietly she closed the door and looked around.

Kira found it hard to sleep. So much was strange.

Only the moon was familiar. Tonight it was almost full, flooding her new living space with silvery light through the glass of her windows. On such a night back in her other life, in the windowless cott with her mother, she might have risen to enjoy the moonlight. On some moonlit nights she and her mother slipped outside and stood together in the breeze, slapping at mosquitoes and watching the clouds slide past the bright globe in the night sky.

Here, through a slightly opened window, night breeze and moonlight entered her room together. The moonlight slipped over the table in the corner and washed across the polished wooden floor. She saw her sandals paired beside the chair where she had sat to remove them. She saw her walking stick leaning in the corner, its shadow outlined on the wall.

She saw the shapes of the objects on the table, the things that Matt had brought, bundled, to her. She wondered how he had chosen. Perhaps it had been rushed, with the fire starting; perhaps he had simply grabbed what he could with his impetuous, generous small hands.

There was her threading frame. She thanked Matt in her mind. He had known what the frame meant to her.

Dried herbs in a small basket. Kira was glad to have those and hoped she could remember which was to be used for what. Not that the herbs had been of any value to her mother when the terrible sickness came; but for the small things, an ache in the shoulder, a bite that festered and swelled, the herbs were helpful then. And she was happy to have the basket. She remembered her mother weaving it from river grass.

Some chunky tubers. Kira smiled, picturing Matt grabbing food, probably nibbling while he was at it. She would not need those now. The meal brought to her on a tray in the evening had been hearty: thick bread and a soup made of meat and barley with greens throughout, and flavored strongly with herbs she savored but didn't recognize. She had eaten it from a glazed earthen bowl, using a spoon carved from bone, and then wiped her mouth and hands with a folded fine-woven cloth.

No meal had ever been so elegant for Kira. Or so lonely.

In the little arrangement of things were folded pieces of her mother's clothing: a thick shawl with a fringe at the edge, and a skirt, stained from the dyes her mother used, so that the simple, unadorned fabric seemed decorated with streaks of color. Sleepily thinking of her mother's stained skirt, Kira imagined how she could use her threads to outline the bright streaks of color so that with skill — and time; it would take time — she could re-create it into a costume suitable for some celebration.

Not that there had ever been anything for her to celebrate. But maybe this — her new quarters, her new job, the fact that her life had been spared.

Kira tossed restlessly on the bed. She felt an object at her neck. It too had been in the bundle that Matt brought, and she treasured it most of the things he had saved. It was the pendant that her mother had always worn dangling from a leather thong, not visible under her clothing. Kira knew of it, had touched and stroked it often as a small tyke still breastfed. It was a shiny section of rock, split cleanly down one side but studded with shiny purple on the other and with a hole to allow for the thong. A simple but unusual thing, it had been a gift from Kira's father, and Katrina had cherished it as a kind of talisman. Kira had lifted it from her mother's neck when she was ill in order to wash the fevered body, and had placed it on the shelf near the basket of herbs. Matt must have found it there.

Wearing it now around her own neck, Kira lifted it against her cheek, hoping to recapture a feeling of her mother, perhaps the smell of her: herbs and dyes and dried blossoms. But the little rock was inert and odorless, without a hint or memory of life.

In contrast, the scrap of cloth from Kira's pocket, the one which had created itself so magically in her fingers, fluttered where it lay near her head. Perhaps the night breeze through the open window had made it move. For a moment Kira, watching the moonlight and thinking of her mother, didn't notice. Then she saw the cloth tremble slightly, as if it had life, in the pale light. She smiled and the thought crossed her mind that it was like Matt's little dog, looking up, twitching its ears, wagging its woeful tail, hoping to be noticed.

She reached out and touched the cloth. Feeling its warmth in her hand, Kira closed her eyes.

A cloud shadowed the moon, and the room darkened. Finally, she slept, without dreams; and in the morning when Kira woke the little cloth was limp, no more than a wrinkled scrap of pretty fabric in her bed.

7

An egg! That was a treat. In addition to the boiled egg, her breakfast tray contained more of the thick bread and a bowl of warm cereal swimming in cream. Kira yawned and ate.

Usually at waking she and her mother had walked to the stream. Here, she supposed, the green-tiled room took its place. But Kira was nervous about the room. She had entered it the night before and turned the various gleaming handles. Some of the water was hot and startled her. It must be for cooking. Somewhere below, a fire had apparently been built. Somehow the cooking water had been hoisted here, but what was she to do with it? There was no need for her to cook, Kira thought this morning as she had last night. Warm prepared food had been brought.

Mystified still, Kira turned her attention this morning to the long, low tub. Jamison had suggested that she could wash Matt there. There was something that looked and smelled like soap. Leaning forward over the tub's rim, she tried to wash but the procedure was awkward and unnatural; it was easier in the stream. And she could wash her clothes in the stream and hang them on the bushes. Here in this small, windowless room there was no place to dry anything. No breeze. No sun.

It was interesting, Kira decided, that they had found a way for water to enter the building, but impractical and unsanitary, and there was no place to bury waste. She wiped the cold water from her face and hands with the cloth she found in the tiled room and decided that she would return to the stream each day to attend to her needs properly.

She dressed quickly, laced her sandals, pulled the wooden comb through her long hair, grabbed her stick, and hurried through the empty corridor to leave her new home and go for a morning walk. But before she had gone very far, a door in the corridor opened. A boy she recognized emerged and spoke to her.

"Kira the Threader," he said. "They told me you had come."

"You're the Carver," she said. "Jamison told me you were here."

"Yes, I'm Thomas." He grinned at her. He seemed about her age, not long into two syllables, and was a good-looking boy with clear skin and bright eyes. His hair was thick and reddish-brown. A chip in one front tooth showed when he smiled.

"This is where I live," he explained. He opened the door wider so that she could see inside. His room was just like hers, though on this, the opposite side of the corridor, his window view was to the wide central square. She noticed too that his room seemed more of a lived-in place. His things were strewn around.

"This is my workroom too." He gestured, and she could see a large table with his carving tools and scraps of wood. "And there's a storage room, for supplies." He pointed.

"Yes, mine's the same," Kira told him. "My supply room has lots of drawers. I haven't started work yet, but there's a table under the windows, and the light is good there. I think that's where I'll do the threading.

"And there — that door? That's your cooking water and your tub?" Kira asked him. "Do you use it? It seems such a bother, when the stream's so nearby."

"The tenders will show you how it works," he explained.

"Tenders?"

"The one who brought your food? That's a tender. They'll help you however you want. And a guardian will be checking on you every day."

Good. Thomas seemed to know how things worked. It would be a help, Kira thought, because it all seemed so new, so foreign. "Have you lived here a long time?" she asked politely.

"Yes," he replied. "Since I was quite young."

"How did it happen that you came here?"

The boy frowned, thinking back. "I had just begun carving. I was a very little tyke, but somehow

I had discovered that if I took a sharp tool and a piece of wood, I could make pictures.

"Everyone thought it was quite amazing." He laughed. "I guess it was."

Kira laughed a little too, but she was remembering herself, very small, finding that her fingers had a kind of magic to them when she held the colored threads, seeing her mother's astonishment and the look on the face of the Guardian. It must have been the same, she thought, for this boy.

"Somehow the Guardians heard about my work. They came to our cott and admired it."

So similar, Kira thought.

"Then," Thomas continued, "not long after, my parents were both killed during a storm. Struck by lightning, both at once."

Kira was shocked. She had heard of *trees* felled by lightning. But not people. The people didn't go out during thunderstorms. "Were you there? How did you stay safe?"

"No, I was alone at the cott. My parents were doing an errand of some sort. I remember that a messenger had been sent for them. But then some guardians came and got me and told me of their deaths. It was fortunate that they knew of me and felt that my work was of value, even though I was still small. Otherwise, I would have simply been given away. But instead, they brought me here.

"I've been here ever since." He gestured around

the room. "For a long time I practiced, and learned. And I've made ornaments for many of the guardians. Now, though, I do real work. Important work." He pointed, and she could see that a long piece of wood was resting against the table, leaning in the same way that she leaned her walking stick. But this stick was intricately decorated, and from the shavings on the table she could tell that the boy had been working on it.

"They've given me wonderful tools," Thomas told her.

Outside, the bell rang. Kira was disconcerted. Back in the cott, the sound of the bell meant that it was time to go to work. "Should I go back to my quarters?" she asked. "I was going to walk to the stream."

Thomas shrugged. "It doesn't matter. You can do whatever you want. There are no real rules. Only that you are required to do the work you were brought here for. They'll check on your work every day.

"I'm going out now to visit my mother's sister. She has a new tyke. A girl. Look! I'm taking a toy." He reached into his pocket and showed Kira an intricately carved bird. It was hollow; he held it to his mouth and made it whistle. "I made it yesterday," he explained. "It took time from my regular work, but not much. It was easy to do.

"I'll be back for lunch," he added, "because I

have work to do this afternoon. Shall I bring my lunch tray to your quarters so that we can eat together?"

Kira agreed happily.

"And look," he said, "here comes the tender who'll pick up the morning trays. She's very nice. You ask her — No, wait. I'll ask her."

While Kira watched curiously, Thomas approached the tender and spoke briefly to her. She nodded.

"You follow her back to your quarters, Kira," Thomas said. "You don't need to go to the stream. She'll explain the bathroom to you. See you at lunch!" He put the little carved bird into his pocket, closed the door to his room, and headed down the corridor. Kira followed the tender back the way she had come.

Jamison came to her room shortly after lunch. Thomas had eaten and hurried away to his quarters to resume work. Kira had just gone into the small room lined with drawers and slid open the one containing the Singer's robe. She had not yet unfolded it. She had never been permitted to touch it before and was in awe now and a little nervous. She was staring down at the lavishly decorated fabric, remembering her mother's deft hands holding the bone needle, when she heard the knock on her door and then heard Jamison come in.

"Ah," he said. "The robe."

"I was thinking that I must soon begin my duties," Kira told him, "but I'm almost afraid to start. This is so new to me."

He lifted the robe from the drawer and carried it to the table by the window. There in the light the colors were even more magnificent and Kira felt even more inadequate.

"Are you comfortable here? You slept well? They brought your food? It was good?"

So many questions. Kira considered whether to tell him how restlessly she had slept and decided against it. She glanced at the bed to see if the bed coverings would reveal her tossing and noticed for the first time that someone, probably the tender who brought and took away the food, had smoothed everything so that there was no sign that the bed had been used at all.

"Yes," she told Jamison. "Thank you. And I met Thomas the Carver. He ate his lunch with me. It was nice to have someone to talk to.

"And the tender explained things I needed to know," she added. "I thought the hot water was for cooking. I never used hot water just for washing before."

He wasn't paying attention to her embarrassed explanation about the bathroom. He was looking carefully at the robe, sliding his hand across the fabric. "Your mother made minor repairs each year. But now it must all be restored. This is your job."

Kira nodded. "I understand," she said, though she didn't, not really.

"This is the entire story of our world. We must keep it intact. *More* than intact." She saw that his hand had moved and was stroking the wide unadorned section of fabric, the section of the cloth that fell across the Singer's shoulders. "The future will be told here," he said. "Our world depends upon the telling.

"Your supplies? They are adequate? There is much to be done here."

Supplies? Kira remembered that she had brought a basket of her own threads. Looking now at the magnificent robe, she knew that her sparse collection, a few leftover colored threads that her mother had allowed her to use for her own, was not adequate at all. Even if she had the skill — and she was not at all certain that she did — she could never restore the robe with what she had brought. Then she remembered the drawers that she had not yet opened.

"I haven't looked yet," she confessed. She went to the shallow drawers that he had pointed out to her yesterday. They were filled with rolled white threads in many different widths and textures. There were needles of all sizes and cutting tools laid neatly in a row.

Kira's heart sank. She had hoped that perhaps the threads would already be dyed. Glancing back at the robe on the table, at its wide array of hues, she felt overwhelmed. If only her mother's threads had been saved! But they were gone, all burned.

She bit her lip and looked nervously at Jamison. "They're not colored," she murmured.

"You said your mother had been teaching you to dye," he reminded her.

Kira nodded. She *had* implied that, but it had not been completely true. Her mother had *planned* to teach her. "I still have much to learn," she confessed. "I learn quickly," she added, hoping that it didn't sound vain.

Jamison looked at her with a slight frown. "I will send you to Annabella," he told her. "She is far in the woods, but the path is safe, and she can finish the teaching that your mother started.

"The Ruin Song is not until autumn-start," he pointed out. "That's still several months away. The Singer won't need the robe until then. You'll have plenty of time."

Kira nodded uncertainly. Jamison had been her defender. Now it seemed he was her adviser. Kira was grateful for his help. Still, she sensed an edge, an urgency, to his voice that had not been there before.

When he left her room, after pointing out a cord on the wall that she could pull if she needed anything, Kira looked again at the robe displayed on the table. So many colors! So many shades of each color! Despite his reassurance, autumn-start was not that far away.

Today, Kira decided, she would examine the robe

and plan. Tomorrow, first thing, she would find Annabella and plead for help.

8

Matt wanted to come.

"You be needing me and Branch for protectors," he said. "Them woods is full of fierce creatures."

Kira laughed. "Protectors? You?"

"Me and Branchie, us is tough," Matt said. He flexed what passed for muscles in his scrawny arms. "I only *look* wee."

"Jamison said it was safe as long as we stay on the path," Kira reminded the boy. Secretly, she thought it would be fun to have both of them, boy and dog, for company.

"But suppose you was to get lost," Matt said. "Me and Branch can find our way out of anywheres. You be needing us for certain iffen you get lost."

"But I'll be gone all day. You'll get hungry."

Triumphantly Matt pulled a thick wad of bread from the voluminous pocket of his baggy shorts. "Filched this crustie from the baker," he announced with pride.

So the boy won, to Kira's delight, and she had company for the journey into the forest.

It was about an hour's walk. Jamison was correct; there seemed to be no danger. Although thick trees shaded the path and they could hear rustling in the undergrowth and unfamiliar cries of strange forest birds, nothing seemed threatening. Now and then Branch chased a small rodent or nosed about an opening in the earth, frightening whatever small animal made its home there.

"Probably there be snakies all in here," Matt told her with a mischievous smile.

"I'm not afraid of snakes."

"Most girls be."

"Not me. There were always small snakes in my mother's garden. She said they were friends to the plants. They ate bugs."

"Like Branchie. Look, he catched him one now." Matt pointed. His dog had pounced upon an unlucky creature with long thin legs. "That be called a daddy longlegs."

"Daddy longlegs?" Kira laughed. She'd not heard the name before. "Do you have a father?" she asked the boy curiously.

"Nah. Did onct. But now, me mum is all I got."

"What happened to your father?"

He shrugged. "Dunno.

"In the Fen," he added, "things is different. Many gots no pa. And them that gots them, they be scairt of them, 'cause they hit something horrid.

"Me mum hits too," he added, with a sigh.

"I had a father. He was a fine hunter," Kira told

78

him proudly. "Even Jamison said so. But my father was taken by beasts," she explained.

"Aye, I heared that." She could see that Matt was trying to look sad for her benefit, but it was difficult for a boy whose temperament was so merry. Already he was pointing at a butterfly, gleeful at the bright spotted orange of its wings in the dim forest light.

"See this? You brought it with my mother's things, remember?" She lifted the rock pendant from the neck of her shift.

Matt nodded. "It be all purply. And shiny-like."

Kira dropped it back gently inside her clothing. "My father made it as a gift for my mother."

Matt wrinkled his face, thinking that over. "Gift?" he asked.

Kira was startled that he didn't understand. "When you care about someone and give them something special. Something that they treasure. That's a gift."

Matt laughed. "In the Fen, they don't have that," he said. "In the Fen, iffen they give you something special, it be a kick in your buttie.

"But that's a pretty thing you got," he added politely. "You be lucky I saved it."

It was a long journey for Kira, dragging her twisted leg. Her stick caught at roots knotted under the earth of the path, and she stumbled from time to time. But she was accustomed to the awkwardness and the ache. They had always been with her.

Matt had run ahead with Branch, and they returned to her, excited, announcing that the destination was just around the next curve.

"A wee cott it is!" he called. "And there's the crone outside in the garden, with her crookedy hands full of rainbow!"

Kira hurried along, rounded the curve, and understood what he meant. In front of the tiny hut, a bent and white-haired old woman was working near a lush flower garden. She leaned toward a basket on the ground, lifted handfuls of bright-colored yarns — yellow of various shades, from the palest lemon to a deep tawny gold — and hung them across a rope that was strung from one tree to another. Deeper shades of rust and red were already hanging there.

The woman's hands were gnarled and stained. She lifted one in greeting. She had few teeth and her skin was folded into wrinkles, but her eyes were unclouded. She walked nearer to them, gripping a cane made of wood and seeming unsurprised by the sudden visitors. She peered intently at Kira's face. "You liken your mum," she said.

"You know who I am?" Kira asked, puzzled. The old woman nodded.

"My mother has died."

"Aye. I knowed it."

How? How did you know? But Kira didn't ask.

"I'm called Kira. This is my friend. His name is Matt."

Matt stepped forward, suddenly a little shy. "I

brung my own crustie," he said. "Me and my doggie, we be no trouble to you."

"Sit," the woman named Annabella said to Kira, ignoring Matt and Branch, who was busily sniffing the garden, looking for the right place to lift his stubby leg. "Doubtless you be weary and pained." She gestured toward a low flattened tree stump, and Kira sank down gratefully, rubbing her aching leg. She unlaced her sandals and emptied them of pebbles.

"You must learn the dyes," the old woman said. "You come for that, aye? Your mum did, and she was to teach you."

"There wasn't time." Kira sighed. "And now they want me to know it all, and do the work — the repairing of the Singer's Robe? You know about that?"

Annabella nodded. She returned to the drying-rope and finished hanging the yellow strands. "I can give you some threads," she said, "to start the repair. But you must learn the dyes. There are other things they'll want of you."

Kira thought again of the untouched expanse across the back and shoulders of the robe. It was what they would want of her, to fill that space with future.

"You must come here each day. You must learn all the plants. Look —" The woman gestured at the garden plot, thick with thriving plants, many in summer-start bloom.

"Bedstraw," she said, pointing to a tall plant

81

massed with golden blossoms. "The roots give good red. Madder's better for reds, though. There's my madder over behind." She pointed again, and Kira saw a sprawling, weedy plant in a raised bed. "'Tis the wrong time to take the madder roots now. Fall-start's better, when it lies dormant."

Bedstraw. Madder. I must remember these. I must know these.

"Dyer's greenweed," the woman announced, poking with her cane at a shrub with small flowers. "Use the shoots for a fine yellow. Don't move it, though, lessen you must. Greenweed don't want to transplant."

Greenweed. For yellow.

Kira followed the woman as she rounded a corner of the garden. Annabella stopped and poked at a clumped plant with stiff stems and small oval leaves. "Here's a tough fellow," she said, almost affection-ately. "Saint Johnswort, he's called. No blooms yet; it's too early for him. But when he blooms, you can get a lovely brown from his blossoms. Stain your hands though." She held her own up and cackled with laughter.

Then: "You'll be needing greens. Chamomile can give you that. Water it good. But take just the leaves for your green color. Save the blossoms for tea."

Kira's head was already spinning with the effort to remember the names of the plants and the colors they would create, and only a small corner of the lav-ish garden had been described. Now at the sound of the word water and also tea she realized that she was thirsty.

"Please, do you have a well? Might I have a drink?" she asked.

"And Branchie too? He been looking for a stream but found nought." Matt's voice piped beside Kira; she had almost forgotten that he was there.

Annabella led them to her well behind the cott, and they drank gratefully. Matt poured water into the crevice of a curved rock for his dog, who lapped eagerly and waited for more.

Finally they sat together in the shade, Kira and the old woman, Annabella. Matt, gnawing his bread, wandered off with Branch at his heels.

"You must come each day," Annabella repeated. "You must learn all the plants, all the colors. As your mum did when she was a girl."

"I will. I promise."

"She said you had the knowledge in your fingers. More than she did."

Kira looked at her hands, folded in her lap. "Something happens when I work with the threads. They seem to know things on their own, and my fingers simply follow."

Annabella nodded. "That be the knowledge. I got it for the colors but never for the threads. My hands was always too coarse." She held them up, stained and misshapen. "But to use the knowledge of the threading, you must learn the making of the shades. When to sadden with the iron pot. How to bloom the colors. How to bleed."

To sadden. To bloom. To bleed. What a strange set of words.

"And the mordants too. You must learn those. Sometimes sumac. Tree galls are good. Some lichens.

"Best is — here, come; let me show you. See you make a guess to its birthplace, this mordant." With surprising agility for a woman of four-syllable age, Annabella rose and led Kira to a covered container near the place where a large kettle of dark water, too huge for cooking food, hung above the smoldering remains of an outdoor fire.

Kira leaned forward to see, but when Annabella lifted the lid, she jerked her head back in unpleasant surprise. The smell of the liquid was terrible. Annabella laughed, a delighted cackle.

"Got you a guess?"

Kira shook her head. She couldn't imagine what was in the foul-smelling container or what its origin might be.

Annabella replaced the lid, still laughing. "You save it and age it good," she said. "Then it brings the hue to life and sets it firm.

"It's old piss!" she explained with a satisfied chuckle.

Late in the day, Kira set out for home with Matt and Branch. The bag she carried over her shoulder was filled with colored threads and yarns that Annabella had given to her.

"These'll do for you now," the old dyer had said.

"But you must learn to make your own. Say back to me now, those you keep in mind."

Kira closed her eyes, thought, and said them aloud. "Madder for red. Bedstraw for red too, just the roots. Tops of tansy for yellow, and greenwood for yellow too. And yarrow: yellow and gold. Dark hollyhocks, just the petals, for mauve."

"*Snotweed,*" Matt said loudly with a grin and wiped his own runny nose on his dirty sleeve.

"Hush, you," Kira said to him, laughing. "Don't play foolish now. It's important I remember."

"Broom sedge," she added, still remembering. "Goldy yellows and browns. And Saint Johnswort for browns too, but it'll stain my hands.

"And bronze fennel — leaves and flowers; use them fresh — and you can eat it too. Chamomile for tea and for green hues.

"That's all I remember now," Kira said apologetically. There had been so many others.

Annabella nodded in approval. "It's a starting," she said.

"Matt and I must go or it will become dark before we're back," Kira said, turning. Looking at the sky to assess the time, she suddenly remembered something.

"Can you make blue?" she asked.

But Annabella frowned. "You need the woad," she said. "Gather fresh leaves from first year's growth of woad. And soft rainwater; that makes the blue." She shook her head. "I have nought. Others

85

do, but they be far away."

"Who be others?" Matt asked.

The old woman didn't answer the boy. She pointed toward the far edge of her garden, where the woods began and there seemed to be a narrow overgrown path. Then she turned toward her hut. Kira heard her speak in a low voice. "I ne'er could make it," she was saying. "But some have blue yonder."

9

The Singer's robe contained only a few tiny spots of ancient blue, faded almost to white. After her supper, after the oil lamps had been lit, Kira examined it carefully. She lay her threads — the ones from her own small collection and the many others that Annabella had given to her — on the large table, knowing she would have to match the hues carefully in daylight before she began the repairs. It was then that she noticed — with relief because she would not know how to repair it; and with disappointment because the color of sky would have been such a beautiful addition to the pattern — that there was no real blue any more, only a hint that there once had been.

She said the names of the plants over and over aloud, trying to make a chant of them for easier memory. "Hollyhock and tansy; madder and bedstraw . . ." But they fell into no comfortable rhythm and did not rhyme.

Thomas knocked at her door. Kira greeted him happily, showed him the robe and threads, and told him of her day with the old dyer.

"I can't remember all the names," she said in frustration. "But I'm thinking that if in the morning I go back to where my old cott was, maybe my mother's garden plants, the ones she used for colors, will still be there. And then, seeing them, the names will mean more. I only hope Vandara —"

She paused. She had not told the carver about her enemy, and even saying the name made her apprehensive.

"The woman with the scar?" Thomas asked.

Kira nodded. "Do you know her?"

He shook his head. "But I know who she is," he said. "Everyone does."

He picked up a little skein of the deep crimson. "How did the dyer make this?" he asked curiously.

Kira thought. *Madder for red.* "Madder," she recalled. "Just the roots."

"Madder," he repeated. Then an idea occurred to him. "I could write the names for you, Kira," he suggested. "It would make the remembering easier."

"You can write? And read?"

Thomas nodded. "I learned when I was young. Boys can, the ones who are chosen. And some of the carving I do has words."

"But I can't. So even if you were to write the names, I couldn't read them. And it's not permitted for girls to learn."

"Still, I could help you in the remembering. If you told them to me and I wrote them, then I could read them to you. I know it would help."

She realized he was probably right. So he brought pen and ink and paper from his quarters, and once again she said the words, those she could recall. In the flickering light, she watched as he carefully wrote them down. She saw how the curves and lines in combinations made the sounds, and that he was then able to say them back to her.

When he read the word *hollyhock* aloud with his finger on the word, she saw that it was long, with many lines like tall stems. She turned her eyes away quickly so that she would not learn it, would not be guilty of something clearly forbidden to her. But it made her smile, to see it, to see how the pen formed the shapes and the shapes told a story of a name.

Very early in the morning Kira ate quickly and then walked to the place where her mother's color garden had been. Few people were up and about yet, at sunrise. She half expected to encounter Matt and Branch, but the paths were mostly empty and the village was still quiet. Here and there a tyke cried and she could hear the soft clucking of chickens. But the noisy clangor of daytime life was yet to come.

Approaching, she could see the pen that was already partly built. It had been only a few days, but the women had gathered thorn bushes and circled them around the remains of the cott where Kira had grown up. The encircled ground was still ashes and rubble. Very soon the thorned fence they were building would enclose the area completely; she supposed they would create some kind of gate, and then they would shove their chickens and their tykes inside. There would be sharp wood pieces and jagged fragments of broken pots. Kira sighed, seeing it. The tykes would be scratched and splintered by scraps of her own destroyed past, but there was nothing she could do. She edged quickly past the wreckage and the half-built fence, and found the remains of her mother's color garden at the edge of the woods.

The vegetable garden was completely stripped, but the flower plot remained though its plants were trampled. Clearly the women, dragging their bushes to build the pen, had simply walked across the area; yet the blossoms continued to bloom and she was awed to see that vibrant life still struggled to thrive despite such destruction.

She named them to herself, those she remembered, and picked what she could, filling the cloth she had brought. Annabella had told her that most of the flowers and leaves could be dried and used later. Some, like bronze fennel, should not. "Use it fresh," Annabella had said of the fennel. You could eat it too. Kira left it where it grew and wondered if the women would know that it could be harvested for food.

A dog barked nearby and now she could hear arguing: a hubby shouting at his wife, a tyke being slapped. The village was waking to its routine. It was time for her to go. This was not her place any more.

Kira gathered the cloth around the plants she had

collected and tied the edges together. Then she slung it over her shoulder, picked up her walking stick, and hurried away. On a back path, avoiding the central lane of the village, Kira saw Vandara and averted her eyes. The woman called her name in a smug, taunting voice. "Liking your new life?" she called, and followed the question with a harsh laugh. Quickly Kira turned a corner to escape a confrontation, but the memory of the sarcastic question and the woman's smirk accompanied her home.

"I'll need a place to grow a color garden," she told Jamison hesitantly a few days later, "and an airy place for drying the plants. Also a place where a fire can be built, and pots for the dyeing." She thought some more then added, "And water."

He nodded and said that such things could be provided.

He came each evening to her quarters to assess her work and to ask her needs. It seemed strange to Kira that she could make requests and to have them answered.

But Thomas said it had always been so for him, too. The kinds of wood — ash, heartwood, walnut, or curly maple — each had been brought when he asked. And they had given him tools of all sorts, some he had not known of before.

The days, busy ones, tiring ones, began to pass.

One morning as Kira prepared to go to the dyer's hut, Thomas came to her room.

"Did you hear anything last night?" he asked her uncertainly. "Maybe a sound that woke you?"

Kira thought. "No," she told him. "I slept soundly. Why?"

He seemed puzzled, as if he were trying to remember something. "I thought I heard something, a sound like a child crying. I thought it woke me. But maybe it was a dream. Yes, I guess it was a dream."

He brightened and shrugged off the little mystery. "I've made something for you," he told her. "I've been doing it in the early mornings," he explained, "before I started my regular work."

"What is your usual work, Thomas?" Kira asked. "Mine's the robe, of course. But what have they set you to do?"

"The Singer's staff. It's very old, and his hands — and the hands of other Singers in the past, I suppose — have worn the carvings down so it must all be recarved. It's difficult work. But important. The Singer uses the carvings of the staff to find his place, to remind him of the sections in *the Song*. And there's a large place at the top that has never been carved. Eventually I'll be doing that, carving it for the first time, making my own designs." He laughed. "Not my own, really. They'll tell me what to put there.

"Here." Shyly, Thomas reached into his pocket and handed her the gift. He had made her a small box with a tight fitting lid, its top and sides intricately carved in the pattern of the plants she was beginning to learn and to know. She examined it with delight. She recognized the tall spikes of yarrow and its dense clustered blossoms; around them twined the flopping stems of coreopsis, above a carved base of that plant's mounded dark and feathery leaves.

She knew instantly what she wanted to place in the exquisite box. The small scrap of decorated cloth that she had carried in her pocket on the day of the trial and that comforted her loneliness when she held it before sleeping, was hidden away in one of the drawers that contained supplies. She no longer carried it with her because she feared losing it during her long walks through the woods and her long days hard at work with the dyer.

Now, with Thomas watching, she fetched the scrap and laid it in the box.

"It's a lovely thing," he said, seeing the small cloth.

Kira stroked it before she closed the lid. "It speaks to me somehow," she told him. "It seems almost to have life." She smiled, embarrassed, because she knew it was an odd thing and that he would not understand and could perhaps find her foolish.

But Thomas nodded. "Yes," he said to her surprise. "I have a piece of wood that does the same. One I carved long ago, when I was just a tyke.

"And sometimes I feel it in my fingers still, the knowledge that I had then."

He turned to leave.

That you had then? No more? The knowledge

doesn't stay? Kira was dismayed at the thought but she said nothing to her friend.

Though there was still so much information she needed to acquire from Annabella, Kira was forced to make her learning time at the dyer's cott shorter because it was important to begin to work on the Singer's robe and she needed the daylight. She was glad now of the tiled bathroom that had caused her such confusion at first. The warm water and soap helped to rid her hands of stains, and it was vital that her hands be clean when she touched the robe.

She still had her small frame, the one that Matt had saved from the fire, but there was no need of it. Among the supplies provided for her was a fine new frame that unfolded and stood on sturdy wooden legs so that it was not necessary to hold it in her lap. She placed the frame by the window so she could sit in a chair beside it while she worked.

She spread out the robe on the large table to examine it carefully and select the place where she should begin her work. Now, for the first time, Kira began to perceive the vastness from which the Singer created his song. The entire history of the people, culminating with the horrifying story of the Ruin, was portrayed with immense complexity on the voluminous folds of the robe.

Kira could see pale green sea, and in its depths fish of all kinds, some larger than men, larger than ten men together. Then the sea blended imperceptibly into sweeping areas of land populated only by the figures of animal life unknown to her, hulking creatures grazing on tall tan grasses. All of this was only one small corner of the Singer's robe. As her eyes moved along, she saw that out of the pale sea, near the grazing land, rose other land, and on this land appeared men. The tiny stitches created figures of hunters with spears and weaponry, and she saw that little knots of red *(madder for red. Just the roots)* had been used to color blood on the figures of fallen men, those taken by beasts.

She thought of her father. But this scene was long ago, long before her father, long before any of their people. The lifeless men dotted with the red knots of blood were still an infinitesimal section of the robe, a blink of an eye, forgotten now except for the once-a-year Song, the time that the Singer reminded them of the past.

Looking at the robe, and smoothing it with her washed hand, Kira sighed and realized that she did not have time for such study. There was important work to be done, and she had noticed Jamison's increasing sense of urgency. Again and again he came to her room, checking, making certain that she was attentive to her job and would be meticulous in the work.

Identifying a place on one sleeve that badly needed repair, Kira moved that section of the robe into the frame, which held it taut. Then, carefully, using the delicate cutting tools she had been given, Kira snipped away the frayed threads. There was a small stain across an intricately threaded flower in shades of gold, part of a landscape that portrayed rows of tall sunflowers near a pale green stream. Someone long ago — someone skilled in the art — had made the stream appear to flow by stitching white curving lines that gave a sense of foam. How gifted the earlier threader had been! But those stained threads would need to be replaced.

The work was painstakingly slow. Her mother, though her fingers had not had the almost-magical knowledge that Kira's had, would have been more experienced, more deft, and faster.

She held the new gold threads to the window and examined the subtle shifts in hue, choosing just the right ones for the repair.

When the late afternoon light began to dim, Kira stopped work. She looked at the few inches in the frame, assessing what she had accomplished, and decided that she was doing well. Her mother would have been pleased. Jamison would be pleased. She hoped that when the time came to don the Robe, the Singer would be satisfied as well.

But her fingers ached. Kira rubbed them and sighed. This was not at all the same as her own threadings, the small pieces she had done throughout her childhood. It was certainly not like the special one that had begun to move of its own volition in her hand beside her mother's deathbed, to twist and mix the threads in ways she had never learned, to form patterns she had never seen. Her hands had never tired then.

Thinking of that special scrap, Kira went to the carved box, unfolded the bit of cloth, and put it in her pocket. It felt familiar and welcome there, as if a friend had come to visit.

It was almost time for her evening meal to be brought. Kira covered the spread-out robe with a plain cloth to protect it. Then she went along the corridor and knocked on Thomas's door.

The young carver was also just finishing his work. When he called "Come in!" Kira entered and saw that he was wiping the blades of his tools and putting them away. The long staff lay across his worktable, held in a clamp. He smiled when he saw her. They had begun to eat their evening meal together each night.

"Listen," Thomas said, and pointed to his windows. She could hear noise coming from the central plaza below. Her own room, facing the forest, was always quiet.

"What's happening?"

"Take a look. They're preparing for a hunt tomorrow."

Kira moved to the window and looked down. Below, the men were gathering for the distribution of weapons. Hunts always began early in the morning; the men left the village before sunrise. But this was preparation. Kira could see that doors had been opened in an outbuilding beside the Council Edifice, and from the storage place long spears were being brought and placed in piles in the center of the plaza.

Men were lifting the spears, testing the weight, looking for the one that felt right. There were arguments. She saw two men with their hands grasping the same spearshaft, each determined to hold on. They were yelling at each other.

In the midst of the noisy chaos, Kira saw a small figure dart in among the men and grab a spear. No one else seemed to notice. They were all absorbed with themselves, shoving and pushing. She saw that one man was already bloodied from a spear point, and it was clear that others would be injured before the disorganized distribution was complete. No one paid any attention to the boy. From her place in the window, Kira watched as the figure, holding an undisputed spear, moved triumphantly to the side of the crowd. A dog scampered by his bare feet.

"It's Matt!" Kira cried in dismay. "He's just a tyke, Thomas! He's much too young for a hunt!" When Thomas came to the window, she pointed. He followed her finger and finally saw Matt where he stood to the side with his spear.

Thomas chuckled. "Sometimes boy tykes do that," he explained. "The men don't care. They let them follow along on the hunt."

"But it's too dangerous for a tyke, Thomas!"

"What do you care?" Thomas seemed genuinely

curious. "They're only tykes. There are too many of them anyway."

"He's my friend!"

He seemed to comprehend then. She saw his face change. He looked down toward the boy with concern. Kira could see that now Matt was encircled by the pack of mischief-makers who were often at his side. They were admiring him as he brandished the spear.

Kira felt a startling sensation — a throbbing in her hip. She reached for it, intending to rub it away, thinking that perhaps she had leaned too hard against the windowsill. Then her hand went instinctively to her pocket. She remembered that she had placed the scrap of cloth there. She touched the fabric and felt tension, danger, and a warning from it.

"Please, Thomas," Kira said urgently, "Help me stop him!"

10

It was difficult to get through the crowd. Kira followed Thomas, who was taller than she, as he pushed to make a path through the shouting, raucous men. She recognized some: the butcher was there, cursing as he argued with another man, and she could see her mother's brother too, in a group comparing the weights of their weapons with loud bragging comments.

Kira had not been much in the world of men. They led very separate lives from those of women. She had never envied them. Now, as she found herself jostled by their thick, sweat-smelling bodies, as she heard their muttered angry comments and their shouts, she found herself both frightened and annoyed. But she realized that this was hunt behavior, a time for flaunting and boasting, a time for testing each other. No wonder Matt, with his childish swagger, wanted to be part of it.

A light-haired man with blood smeared on his arm turned from a shoving match and grabbed at her as she hurried by. "Here's a trophy!" she heard him call out. But his companions were preoccupied with their argument. Using her walking stick as a prod, she pushed the man away and wrenched her wrist free from his grasp.

"You shouldn't be here," Thomas whispered when she caught up with him. They had almost reached the side of the square where they had last spotted Matt. "It's always only men. And at hunt time they act brutish."

Kira knew that. She could tell from the smell, the coarse quarreling, and the noise that it was not a place for girls or women, and she kept her head lowered and her eyes on the ground, hoping not to be noticed and grabbed again.

"There's Branch!" She pointed at the little dog, who recognized her and wagged his crooked stub of a tail. "Matt will be nearby!"

With Thomas beside her, she pushed her way through and found him, still prancing with his spear. Its sharp point was dangerously close to the other tykes.

"Matt!" she called in a scolding voice.

He saw her, waved, and grinned. "I'm Mattie now!" he called.

Exasperated, Kira grabbed the spear shaft just above his hand. "You won't be two syllables for a long time, Matt," she said. "Thomas, take this." She removed the spear from Matt's grasp and handed it carefully to the Carver.

"Yes, I be!" Matt said, laughing and proud. "Looky here! I've got me a manly pelt!"

The little boy raised both arms above his head to show her his joke. Kira looked. His underarms were thick with some kind of growth. "What is that?" she asked him. Then she wrinkled her nose. "It smells terrible!" She touched it, pulled some away, and began to laugh. "Matt, that's swamp grass. It's awful stuff. What do you mean, plastering yourself with it?" She could see that he'd smeared it on his chest as well.

Thomas handed the spear to a man who grabbed it eagerly. He looked down at Matt, who was wiggling under Kira's hands on his shoulders. "You look like a beast-boy! What do you say, Kira? I think it's time we showed Matt the bathroom! Shall we clean him up and wash his second syllable away?"

At the word *wash* Matt wiggled harder, trying to get free. But Thomas and Kira both held him and finally he allowed Thomas to pick him up and carry him on his shoulders, towering over the crowd.

Now that the dangerous fascination of the spear was gone, Matt's group of young admirers dispersed. Kira could hear Matt calling from his perch above the noisy, shoving men, "Looky here at the beast-boy!" No one looked, or cared. She found Branch underfoot and picked him up to keep him safe from so many trampling feet. Carrying the dog tucked under her free arm, Kira leaned on her stick and followed Thomas; they edged their way around the crowd and back into the quiet of the building's corridors.

Kira listened, laughing, to the wails and whimpers as Thomas mercilessly scrubbed both Matt and Branch in his bathroom tub. "Not me hairs too!" Matt howled in protest as Thomas poured water over his tangled mop of hair. "You're drownding me!"

Finally, with Matt pink-faced and subdued, his washed hair toweled into a halo and his clean body wrapped in a blanket, they shared their meal. Branch shook himself briskly as if he had just played in the stream, then settled himself on the floor and nibbled at scraps they handed to him.

Matt sniffed warily at his own hand and grimaced. "That soapie's horrid awful," he said. "But I like the food," he added and filled his plate again.

After dinner Kira brushed his hair while he complained loudly. Then she held a mirror for him. Mirrors had been new to her too when she came here to live, and they gave an image different from the stream reflection that had been all she had known of herself. Matt examined his own image with interest, wrinkling his nose and raising his eyebrows. He showed his teeth, growled at the mirror, and startled Branch, who was sleeping under the table. "I be so fierce," Matt announced smugly. "You would've drownded me but I fought so fierce."

Finally they redressed him in his raggedy clothing. He looked down at himself. Then he reached suddenly for the leather thong around Kira's neck.

"Gimme," he said.

She pulled back, annoyed. "Don't, Matt," she

told him and pulled her necklace loose from his hand. "Don't grab. If you want something, you should ask."

"Gimme is an ask," he pointed out, puzzled.

"No, it isn't. You should learn some manners. Anyway," Kira added, "you can't have it. I told you it was special."

"A gift," Matt said.

"Yes. A gift from my father to my mother."

"So she'd like him best."

Kira laughed. "Maybe so. But she already liked him best."

"I want a gift. I never be having one."

Laughing, Thomas and Kira gave him the smooth bar of soap, which he tucked solemnly into his pocket. Then they turned him loose. By now the men and the spears were gone. They watched from the window as the small figure followed by his dog crossed the deserted plaza and disappeared into the night.

Alone with Thomas, Kira tried to explain the warning that had come to her from the cloth. "It creates a feeling in my hand," she explained hesitantly. "Look." She took it from her pocket and held it toward the light. But it was still now. She could feel a kind of comfort and silence from it, nothing like the tension that had stirred it earlier. But she felt disappointed that it now seemed no more than a scrap of cloth; she wanted Thomas to understand.

She sighed. "I'm sorry," she said. "It seems

lifeless, I know. But there are times —"

Thomas nodded. "Perhaps the feeling is for you alone," he said. "Here, I'll show you my bit of wood." He went to a shelf above the table where he kept his tools and took down a piece of light-colored pine small enough to fit into the palm of his hand. Kira could see that it was intricately decorated with carved designs that interwove around it in complicated curves.

"You carved this when you were just a tyke?" she asked him in surprise. She had never seen anything so extraordinary. The boxes and ornaments that were on his worktable, beautiful in their own way, were much simpler than this small piece.

Thomas shook his head. "I began to," he explained. "I was learning to use the tools. I began to try them on this small chunk of wood that had been discarded. And it —"

He hesitated. He stared at the piece of wood as if it mystified him still.

"It carved itself?" Kira asked.

"It did. It seemed to, at least."

"It was the same for me with the cloth."

"It's why I understand the way the cloth speaks to you. The wood speaks in the same way. I can feel it in my hand. Sometimes it —"

"Warns you?" Kira asked, remembering how the cloth had seemed to tense and tremble when she saw Matt holding the spear.

Thomas nodded. "And calms me," he added.

"When I came here so young, sometimes I was very lonely and frightened. But the feel of the wood was calming."

"Yes, the cloth is soothing at times too. I was fearful here at first, the same as you, when everything was so new. But when I held the scrap, I felt reassured." She thought for a moment, trying to picture what this life in the Edifice must have been like for Thomas, brought here very young.

"I think it's easier for me because I'm not alone, as you were," she told him. "Jamison comes every day to look at my work. And I have you just down the corridor."

The two friends sat silently for a moment. Then Kira replaced the cloth in her pocket and rose from her chair. "I must go to my room," she said. "There's so much to do.

"Thank you for helping me with Matt," she added. "He's a naughty tyke, isn't he?"

Thomas, returning his carved piece to the shelf, agreed with a grin. "Horrid naughty," he said and they laughed together with affection for their little friend.

11

Kira, trembling, hurried into the clearing where Annabella's small house stood.

She was alone this morning. Matt still accompanied her occasionally, but he was bored by the old dyer and her endless instructions. More often he and his dog were off with his friends, dreaming up adventures. Matt was still annoyed about the bath. His mates had laughed at him when they saw him clean.

So this morning Kira made her own way down the forest path. This morning, for the first time, she had been frightened.

"What's wrong?" Annabella was at the outdoor fire. She must have risen before dawn to have the fire so hot by now. It crackled and spat under the huge iron kettle. Yet the sun had barely risen when Kira set out.

Catching her breath, Kira limped past the gardens to where the old woman stood sweating as the heat from the flames pulsed and shimmered in the air. There was an aura of safety here, Kira felt. She willed her body to relax.

"You have a fear look to you," the dyer observed.

"A beast followed me on the path," Kira explained, trying to breathe normally. The panic was beginning to subside but she still felt tense. "I could hear it in the bushes. I could hear its steps, and sometimes it growled."

To her surprise, Annabella chuckled. The old woman had always been kind to her and patient. Why would she laugh at her fear?

"I can't run," Kira explained, "because of my leg."

"No need of running," Annabella said. She stirred the water in the pot, which was beginning to show occasional small bubbles at the surface. "We'll boil coneflowers for a brownish green," she said. "Just the flower heads. The leaves and stems make gold." With a nod of her head, she indicated a filled sack of flower heads on the ground nearby.

Kira picked up the sack. When Annabella, testing the water with her stick, nodded, she emptied the massed blossoms into the pot. Together they watched as the mixture began to simmer. Then Annabella laid her stirring stick on the ground.

"Come inside," the old woman said. "I'll give you tea for calming." From a nearby, smaller fire, she lifted a kettle from its hook and carried it into the cott.

Kira followed her. She knew the flower heads would have to boil till midday and then remain steeping in their water for many hours more. Extracting the colors was always a slow process. The coneflower dye-water would not be ready for use until the next morning.

The dyeing yard, affected by the fire, was already sultry and almost oppressive. But inside, the cott was cool, protected by its thick walls. Dried plants, beige and fragile, hung from the ceiling rafters. On a thick wooden table by the window, piles of colored yarns lay ready for sorting. It was part of Kira's learning to name and sort the threads. She went to her place at the sorting table, set her stick against the wall, and sat down. Behind her, Annabella poured water from the kettle over dried leaves that she had placed in two thick mugs.

"This deep brown is from the goldenrod shoots, isn't it?" Kira held the strands to the window light. "It looks lighter than when it was wet. But it's still a fine brown." She had helped the dyer prepare the shoots for their dye-bath a few days before.

Annabella brought the mugs to the table. She glanced at the strands in Kira's hand and nodded. "The goldenrod be blossoming soon. We'll use the blossoms fresh, not dried, for brightest yellow. And the blossoms boil only a short time, not as long as the shoots."

More bits of knowledge to grasp and hold in her memory. She would ask Thomas to write them down with the rest. Kira sipped at the strong hot tea and thought again about the ominous stalking sound in the woods.

"I was so frightened on my way here," she confessed. "Truly, Annabella, I can't run at all. My leg's

109

a useless thing." She looked down at it, ashamed.

The old woman shrugged. "It brung you here," she said.

"Yes, and I'm grateful for that. But I move so slowly." Kira stroked the rough side of the earthen mug, thinking. "When Matt and Branch come with me, nothing stalks me. Maybe Matt would let me bring Branch each day. Even a little dog might scare the beasts back."

Annabella laughed. "There be no beasts," she said.

Kira stared at her. Of course no beasts would come to this clearing where fires glowed. And the old woman seemed never to leave the clearing, never to walk the path to the village. "All I need be here," she had told Kira, speaking disdainfully of the village and its noisy life. But still she had lived to be four syllables and had acquired four generations of wisdom. Why did she suddenly sound like an ignorant tyke, pretending that there was no danger? Like Matt, beating his chest with bravado and pasting it thick with swamp grass that he called a manly pelt?

Pretending didn't keep you safe.

"I heard it growl," Kira said in a low voice.

"Name the threads," Annabella commanded.

Kira sighed. "Yarrow," she said and set some pale yellow next to the deep brown. The dyer nodded.

She examined a brighter yellow in the light. "Tansy," she decided finally, and the dyer nodded again.

"It growled," Kira said once more.

"There be no beasts," the dyer repeated firmly.

Kira continued to sort and name the threads. "Madder," she said, stroking the deep red, one of her favorites. She picked up a pale lavender near it and frowned. "I don't know this one. It's pretty."

"Elderberry," the old woman told her. "But it don't stay fast. It don't linger."

Kira folded the lavender threads in her hand. "Annabella," she said finally, "it growled. It *did*."

"Then it be human, playing at beast," Annabella told her in a firm and certain voice. "Meaning to keep you scairt of the woods. There be no beasts."

Together, slowly, they sorted and named the threads.

Later, walking home through a silent forest with no frightening sounds from the thick bushes on either side of the path, Kira wondered what human would have stalked her, and why.

"Thomas," Kira asked as they ate together, "have you ever seen a beast?"

"Not alive."

"You've seen a dead one, then?"

"We all have. When the hunters bring them in. The other night, remember? They brought them in after the hunt. There was a huge pile over by the butcher's yard."

Kira wrinkled her nose, remembering. "What a smell," she said. "But, Thomas —"

111

He waited for her question. Tonight for dinner they had been brought meat in a thick sauce. Beside it on the plate were some small roasted potatoes.

Kira pointed at the meat on her own plate. "*This* is what the hunters brought. It's hare, I think."

He nodded, agreeing.

"Everything the hunters brought in was like this. Wild rabbit. Some birds. There wasn't anything, well, anything very large."

"There were deer. I saw two at the butcher's."

"But deer are gentle, frightened things. The hunters bring nothing with claws or fangs. They never catch anything that could be called a beast."

Thomas shuddered. "Lucky. A beast could kill."

Kira thought of her father. Taken by beasts.

"Annabella says there be none," she confided.

"Be none?" Thomas looked puzzled.

"That's the way she said it. 'There be no beasts.'"

"She speaks like Matt?" Thomas had not met the old dyer.

Kira nodded. "A bit. Perhaps she grew up in the Fen."

They ate in silence for a moment. Finally Kira asked again. "So you've never seen a real beast?"

"No," Thomas acknowledged.

"But probably you know someone who has."

He thought for a moment and then shook his head. "Do you?" he asked.

Kira looked at the table. It had always been hard to talk of it, even to her mother. "My father was taken by beasts," she told him.

"You saw it?" His voice was shocked.

"No. I was not yet born."

"Your mother saw?"

She tried to remember her mother's telling. "No. She didn't. He went on the hunt. Everyone says that he was a fine hunter. But he didn't return. They came to my mother with the news, that he'd been attacked and taken by beasts on the hunt."

She looked at him, puzzled. "Yet Annabella says there be none."

"How could she know?" Thomas asked skeptically.

"She's four syllables, Thomas. Those who live to four syllables know all there is."

Thomas nodded in agreement, then yawned. He had been working hard all day. His tools still lay on the worktable: small chisels with which he had been meticulously recarving, reshaping the worn, smooth places on the elaborate staff that the Singer used. It was painstaking work that allowed for no error. Thomas had told her that often his head ached and he had to stop again and again to rest his eyes.

"I'll go so you can rest," Kira told him. "I must put away my own work before bed."

She returned to her room at the other end of the corridor and folded the robe that still lay on her table. She had worked on the stitchery throughout the afternoon, after her return from the forest. She had shown it to Jamison as she did each day, and he had nodded in approval. Now Kira was tired too. The long walks to the dyer's cott each day were exhausting, but at the same time the fresh air made her feel cleansed and invigorated. Thomas should get outside more, she thought, and then laughed to herself; she sounded like a scolding mother.

After a bath — how she enjoyed the warm water now! — Kira put on the simple nightgown that was provided clean for her each day. Then she went to the carved box and took the scrap of fabric with her to her bed. The fear of the thing in the bushes by the path lingered with her still, and she thought of it as she waited for sleep.

Is it true, that there be no beasts? Her thoughts framed the question, and her mind responded in a whisper to herself as the fabric lay curled warm in the palm of her hand.

There be none.

What of my father, then, him taken by beasts? Kira drifted into sleep, the words gliding slippery from her thoughts. She dreamed the question, her breath soft and even against the pillow.

The fabric gave a kind of answer but it was no more than a flutter, like a breeze across her that she would not remember when she woke at dawn. The scrap told her something of her father — something important, something that mattered — but the knowledge entered her sleep, trembling through like a dream, and in the morning she did not know that it was there at all.

12

When the bell for rising rang, Kira awoke with a sense that something had changed: she had an awareness of a difference, but had forgotten what the difference was. She sat for a moment on the edge of her bed, thinking. But she could not grasp whatever it was and finally stopped trying. Sometimes, she knew, lost memories and forgotten dreams came back more easily if you put them out of your mind.

Outside, it was stormy. Wind shook the trees and blew a sheet of heavy rain against the building. The hard ground below had turned to mud overnight, and it was clear that Kira would not go to the dyer's cott today. Just as well, she thought; there was much work to do on the robe, and autumn-start, the time of the Gathering, was approaching. Recently Jamison had been stopping by sometimes twice a day to see the progress she had made. He seemed pleased by her work.

"Here," he had said to her just the day before yesterday, smoothing his hand across the large undecorated place, "is where you will start your own work. After this year's Gathering, after you've finished with the restoration, you'll have this entire section to work on for years to come."

Kira touched the place where his hand lay. She tried to determine whether her fingers would feel the magic there. But there was only emptiness. There was a feeling of unfilled need.

He seemed to sense her uncertainty and reassured her. "Don't worry," he said. "We will explain to you what we want pictured there."

Kira didn't reply. His reassurance troubled her. It wouldn't be instruction that she needed, it would be the magic to come to her hands.

Remembering the conversation, Kira thought suddenly, *Jamison! I can ask him about the beasts!* He had told her that he had been part of the hunt that day, that he had seen her father's death.

And maybe she would ask Matt too. Wild little thing that he was, Kira had no doubt that Matt had crossed the boundaries often and had gone to places tykes were not supposed to go. She laughed quietly, thinking of Matt and his mischief. He spied on everything, knew everything. Had she and Thomas not stopped him, he would have tagged along with the men on the hunt and put himself in danger. Perhaps he had done it before.

Perhaps he had seen beasts.

When the tender came with the morning meal, Kira asked that the lights be lit. The rainstorm made the room dim, even beside the window where she sat to work. Finally she settled herself with the outspread robe and placed the frame around the newest section waiting to be repaired. As she had often done, she followed with her eyes and fingers the complex story of the world portrayed on the robe: the starting point, long mended now, with the green water, the dark beasts on its shore, and the men bloodied by the hunt. Beyond, villages appeared, with dwellings of all kinds; curving stitches of smoke from fires were threaded with dull purplish grays. It was fortunate that it needed no repair because Kira had no threads to match. She thought they had been dyed with basil and Annabella had told her how difficult the basil was and how badly it stained your hands.

Then complex, whirling patches of fire: oranges, reds, yellows. Here and there on the robe these fires appeared, a repetitive pattern of ruin, and within the intricately stitched patterns of the bright destructive threads of fire, Kira could see figures of humans portrayed: people destroyed, their tiny villages crumbling, and later even larger, much more splendid towns burned and ravished by fiery destruction. In some places on the robe there was a feeling of entire worlds ending. Yet always there would emerge, nearby, new growth. New people.

Ruin. Rebuilding. Ruin again. Regrowth. Kira followed the scenes with her hand as larger and greater cities appeared and larger, greater destruction took place. The cycle was so regular that its pattern took on a clear form: an up-and-down movement, wavelike. From the tiny corner where it began, where the first ruin came, it enlarged upon itself. The fires grew as the villages grew. All of them were still tiny, created from the smallest stitches and combinations of stitches, but she could see their pattern of growth and how each time the ruin was worse and the rebuilding more difficult.

But the sections of serenity were exquisite. Miniature flowers of countless hues flourished in meadows streaked with golden-threaded sunlight. Human figures embraced. The pattern of the peaceful times felt immensely tranquil compared to the tortured chaos of the others.

Tracing with her finger the white and pink-tinged clouds against pale skies of gray or green, Kira wished again for blue. The color of calm. What was it Annabella had said? That they had blue yonder? What did that mean? Who were *they*? And where was *yonder*?

More unanswered questions.

Great sheets of rain spattered against the window, distracting her. Kira sighed and watched the trees bend and sway in the wind. Thunder muttered in the distance.

She wondered where Matt was, what he was doing in this weather. She knew that ordinary people — those who lived near the place where she and her mother had shared their cott — would be indoors today, the men sullen and edgy, the women complaining loudly because weather kept them from their usual chores. Tykes, confined, would be fighting and then wailing in response to swift backhanded slaps from their mothers.

Her own life with her soft-spoken widowed mother had been different. But it had set her apart too and made others, like Vandara, hostile.

"Kira?" She heard Thomas's voice and his knock at her door.

"Come in."

He came and stood by her window, eyeing the rain. "I was just wondering what Matt's up to in this weather," Kira said.

Thomas began to laugh. "Well, I can answer that. He's up to finishing my breakfast. He arrived early this morning, dripping wet. He said his mother threw him out because he was noisy and troublesome. I think he just wanted breakfast though."

"Branch too?"

"Branch too. Of course."

As if in response, they heard the tap-tapping of the dog's feet in the corridor; then Branch appeared in the doorway, his head cocked, ears up, bent tail wagging exuberantly. Kira knelt and scratched behind his ear.

"Kira?" Thomas was still staring through the window at the rain.

"Hmmm?" She looked up from the dog.

"I heard it again in the night. I'm certain of it this time. The sound of a child crying. It seemed to come from the floor below."

She looked at him and saw that he was concerned. "I wonder, Kira," he said hesitantly, "would you go with me? To explore a bit? I suppose it could be just the sound of wind."

It was true that outside the wind was relentless. Tree branches lashed the side of the building and torn leaves whirled away. The sound of the storm, however, was nothing like the sound of a crying child.

"Maybe an animal?" Kira suggested. "I've heard cats yowling so that they sound like babies with colicky bellies."

"Cats?" Thomas repeated dubiously. "Well, maybe."

"Or a young goat? They make a crying sound."

Thomas shook his head. "It wasn't a goat."

"Well, no one ever said we couldn't explore," Kira commented. "Not to me, anyway."

"Nor me."

"All right, then, I'll go with you. The light's not good for working this morning anyway." She stood. Branch wriggled with anticipation. "What about Matt? I suppose we should take him along."

"Take me where?" Matt appeared in the doorway, damp-haired and barefoot with crumbs on his chin, jam on the edges of his mouth, and wearing a too-large woven shirt belonging to Thomas. "Shall we be having an adventure?"

"Matt?" Kira remembered her intention to ask him. "Have you ever seen a beast? A real one?"

Matt's face lighted. "Billions and billions." He made a beast face, teeth exposed. He roared and his

120

dog jumped away from him in alarm.

Kira rolled her eyes and looked at Thomas.

"Here, Branchie." Matt, his beast disguise abandoned, squatted beside the dog, who came forward and sniffed him. "Some smearies for you." He grinned as the dog licked breakfast remains from his face.

"Yes, we'll have ourselves an adventure," Kira told him. She laid the protective cover over the robe. "We thought we'd explore a bit. We've never been on the floor below this one."

Matt eyes widened in delight at the idea of an exploration.

"I heard a noise last night," Thomas explained. "Probably nothing, but we thought we'd go take a look."

"Noise don't never be *nothing*," Matt pointed out. Quite rightly, Kira thought.

"Well, it's probably nothing important," Thomas amended.

"But maybe it be interesting!" Matt said eagerly.

Together, followed by the dog, the three started down the corridor toward the stairs.

13

Usually Branch scampered eagerly back and forth, leading the way, then circling back. This morning he was more cautious and followed behind. The thunder was still grumbling outside, and the hallway was dimly lighted. Thomas led the way. The dog's toenails clicked on the tiles. Matt's bare feet moved silently beside him, and the only other sounds were Kira's walking stick, which made a muted thump with each step, and the dragging of her twisted leg.

Like the floor above, where they lived, this was simply an empty corridor lined with closed wooden doors.

Thomas turned a corner. Then he jumped back as if he had been startled by something. The others, even the dog, froze.

"Shhhh." Thomas gestured for silence with his finger to his mouth.

Ahead, around the corner, they heard footsteps. Then a knock, the opening of a door, and a voice. The voice and the inflection of the words — though the words themselves were not clear — sounded familiar to Kira.

"It's Jamison," she mouthed silently to Thomas. He nodded, agreeing, and peered around the corner.

It occurred to Kira that Jamison had been her defender, had been the one responsible for her being here at all in this new life. So there was really no reason to huddle here in the dim hallway, hiding from him. Yet she was oddly fearful.

She tiptoed forward and leaned beside Thomas. They could see that one of the doors was open. An indistinct murmur of voices came from within. One voice was Jamison's. The other was that of a child.

The child cried briefly.

Jamison spoke.

Then the child, surprisingly, began to sing.

Its clear, high voice soared. No words. Just the voice, almost instrumentlike in its clarity. It rose, leveled at a high note, and hovered there for a long moment.

Kira felt something tug at her clothing. She looked down and saw Matt beside her, wide-eyed, pulling at her skirt. She motioned to him to stay silent.

Then the singing broke off abruptly, and the child cried again.

They heard Jamison's voice. It was harsh now. Kira had never heard him speak in that way.

The door slammed shut, and the voices were muted.

Matt was still tugging at her, and Kira leaned down so that he could whisper what he had to say.

"It's me friend," he said urgently. "Well, not really me friend 'cause me and my mates don't like girl tykes none. But I knowed her. She lived in the Fen."

Thomas was listening too. "The one who was singing?" he asked.

Matt nodded enthusiastically. "Her name be Jo. She always be singing in the Fen. I didn't never hear her cry like that none."

"Shhh." Kira tried to quiet Matt but he had a difficult time whispering. "Let's go back," she suggested. "We can talk in my room."

Branch led now, happy to be retreating and enthusiastic about the possibility of more food back where breakfast had been. Stealthily they climbed the stairs and returned.

Safe in Kira's quarters, Matt perched on the bed with his bare feet dangling and told them about the girl who sang. "She be littler'n me," he said. He jumped briefly to the floor and held his own hand level with his shoulder. "She be about this high. And all the peoples in the Fen? They get so happy, hearing her sing." He climbed back onto the bed; Branch jumped up beside him and curled on Kira's pillow.

"But why is she here?" Kira asked, puzzled.

Matt gave an exaggerated shrug. "She be an orphan now. Her mum and pa, they died," he explained.

"Both of them? At the same time?" Kira and Thomas looked at each other. They both knew loss. But had it happened again? To another tyke?

124

Matt nodded importantly. He liked being the messenger, the bringer of information. "First her mum gets the sickness, and then when draggers take her mum to the Field? And her pa go to watch the spirit?"

Kira and Thomas nodded.

"Well," Matt said, making a dramatically sad face, "her pa be so sad at the Field, sitting there, that he taken a big pointy stick and stab hisself through the heart.

"That's what them all said, anyways," he added, seeing the shocked looks his story had produced.

"But he had a tyke! He had a little girl!" Kira said, finding it unbelievable that a father would do such a thing.

Matt shrugged again. He considered that. "Maybe he didn't like her none?" he suggested. Then after a moment he frowned and said, "But how could he not like her none when she sing so good?"

"And how did she get here?" Thomas asked. "What is she doing here?"

"I been told they give her away to someone who had a craving for more tykes," Matt said.

Kira nodded. "Orphans always go to someone else."

"Unless —" Thomas said slowly.

"Unless what?" Kira and Matt asked together.

He pondered that. "Unless they sing," he said at last.

Jamison came to Kira's room, as he always did, later in the day. Outside, the rain still fell. Matt, undaunted, had gone off with his dog to find his mates, wherever they might be in such weather. Thomas had returned to his own quarters to work, and Kira too with extra lamps lighted by the tender, had settled to her task, stitching carefully throughout the afternoon. The interruption when Jamison knocked on her door was welcome. The tender brought tea and they sat companionably together in the room while the rain spattered against the windows.

As usual, he examined her work carefully. His face was the same creased, pleasant face she had known now for many weeks. His voice was courteous and friendly as together they scrutinized the folds of the outstretched robe.

Yet the memory of the harsh sound of his murmured speech in the room below prevented Kira from asking him about the singing child.

"Your work is very fine," Jamison told her. He leaned forward, looking carefully at the section she had just completed, where she had meticulously matched the subtle differences of several yellows and filled in a background area with tiny knotted stitches that formed a texture. "Better than your mother's, although hers was excellent," he added. "She taught you the stitches?"

Kira nodded. "Yes, most of them." She didn't tell him how others seemed simply to come to her untaught. It seemed boastful to speak of it.

"And Annabella the dyes," she added. "I'm using many of her threads still, but I'm beginning now to make my own when I'm at her cott."

"She knows all there is, the old woman," Jamison said. He looked at Kira's leg with apparent concern. "The walk is not too hard for you? One day we'll have the fire pit and the pots here for you. I'm thinking of preparing a place just below." He gestured toward the window, indicating an area between the building and the edge of the woods beyond.

"No. I'm strong. But —" She hesitated.

"Yes?"

"Sometimes I've been fearful on the path," Kira told him. "The forest is so close all around."

"There is nothing to be afraid of there."

"I do fear beasts," she confessed.

"As you should. But stay on the path always. The beasts will not come near the path." His voice was as reassuring as it had been the day of her trial.

"I heard growling once," Kira confided, shuddering a little at the memory of it.

"There is nothing to fear if you don't stray."

"Annabella said the same thing. She told me there was nothing to fear."

"She speaks with four-syllable wisdom."

"But, Jamison?" For some reason, Kira hesitated to tell him this. Perhaps she didn't want to question the old woman's knowledge. But now, feeling reassured by Jamison's interest and concern, she told him the startling thing that the old dyer had said with such certainty. "She said that there are no beasts."

He looked at Kira oddly. The expression on his face seemed a mixture of astonishment and anger. "No beasts? She said that?"

"'There be no beasts,'" Kira repeated. "She said it just that way, several times."

Jamison laid the section of robe he'd been examining back down on the table. "She's very old," he said firmly. "It's dangerous for her to speak that way. Her mind is beginning to wander."

Kira looked at him dubiously. For weeks now she had worked with the dyer. The lists of plants, the many characteristics of each, the details of the dyeing procedures, so much complex knowledge; all of it was clear and complete. Kira had seen no sign, no hint of a wandering mind.

Might the old woman know something that no one else — even someone with the status of Jamison — knew?

"Have you *seen* beasts?" Kira asked him hesitantly.

"Many, many times. The woods are filled with them," Jamison said. "Never stray past the village limits. Do *not* go beyond the path."

Kira looked at him. His expression was hard to discern, but his voice was firm and certain.

"Don't forget, Kira," he continued, "I saw your father taken by beasts. It was a hideous thing.

Terrible."

Jamison sighed and patted her hand sympathetically. Then he turned to leave. "You are doing a fine job," he said again, appreciatively.

"Thank you," Kira murmured. She put her hand, still feeling his touch, into her pocket. Her special scrap of cloth lay folded there. She felt no comfort from it. As the door closed behind Jamison, she stroked the cloth, seeking its solace, but it seemed to withdraw from her touch, almost as if it were trying to warn her of something.

The rain still fell steadily. Through it, she thought for a moment that she could hear the child sob on the floor below.

14

The sun was shining in the morning but Kira woke groggy after a fitful sleep. Following an early breakfast she tied her sandals carefully, anticipating the walk to Annabella's. Maybe the clear, cooler air after the rain would wake her a bit and make her feel better. Her head ached.

Thomas's door was closed. He was probably still asleep. There were no sounds either from the floor below. Kira made her way out of doors, relishing the breeze that lingered after the storm and was pine-scented from trees that were still glistening and wet. It blew her hair away from her face and the misery of her sleepless night began to subside.

Leaning on her stick, Kira made her way to the place where she ordinarily turned from the village and entered the woods on the path. It was quite near the weaving shed.

"Kira!" A woman's voice called to her from the shed, and she saw that it was Marlena, already at the loom so early.

Kira smiled, waved, and detoured to greet the woman.

"We miss you! Them tykes that clean up for us now are worthless. Horrid lazy! And one stole my lunch yesterday." Marlena scowled her outrage. Her feet slowed on the treadle and Kira knew that she was eager to chat and gossip.

"That be him now, that wicked tyke!"

A familiar wet nose touched Kira's ankle. She reached down to scratch Branch and saw Matt grinning at her from behind the corner of the weaving shed. "You there!" Marlena called angrily and he drew back to hide.

"Marlena," Kira asked, remembering that the weaving woman lived in the Fen, "did you ever know a girl tyke named Jo?"

"Jo?" The woman was still peering toward the shed corner, hoping to catch a glimpse of Matt and scold him. "You there!" she called again, but Matt was too sly and too clever to respond.

"Yes. She used to sing."

"Ah, the singing tyke! Yes, I knowed her. Not her name though. But her singing, we all knowed that! Like a bird, it was."

"What happened to her?"

Marlena shrugged. Her feet began to move slowly again on the treadle. "She be tooken off. They give her off to somebody, I guess. She be orphaned, I heared."

She leaned forward and whispered loudly, "Some said her receive the songs by magic. Nobody teached her. The songs, they just come."

131

Her feet paused. She gestured to Kira to come closer. Furtively, Marlena confided, "I heared that them songs was full of knowledges. She be only a small tyke, you know? But when she singed, she had knowledges of things that wasn't even happened yet!

"I never heared it myself, only heared tell of it."

Marlena laughed and her feet took up the rapid pace on the treadle that caused the rhythmic motion of the loom. Kira nodded goodbye to her and started toward the path.

Matt met her there, appearing from behind a tree where he'd been hiding. Kira glanced back but Marlena was busy at her loom and had forgotten them both.

"Are you coming with me this morning?" she asked Matt. "I thought you found it boring at the dyer's hut."

"You mustn't go today," Matt said solemnly. Then he glanced at his dog and began to laugh. "Looky! Old Branch, him trying to catch him a lizzie!"

Kira looked and laughed too. Branch had chased a small lizard to the base of a tree and was watching, frustrated, as it slithered up the trunk beyond his reach. He stood on his hind legs and his front ones churned in the air. The lizard looked back and a moist stiletto tongue darted in and out. Kira watched for a moment, chuckling, and then turned again to Matt.

"What do you mean, I mustn't go? I missed yesterday because of the rain. She's expecting me."

Matt looked solemn. "She not be expecting nobody. She be gone to the Field right when the sun be coming up. Draggers tooken her. I seen it."

"To the Field? What are you talking about, Matt? She couldn't possibly walk to the Field from her cott! It's too far! She's too old! And she wouldn't want to anyway."

Matt rolled his eyes. "I didn't say she be wanting to! I said they *tooken* her! She be dead!"

"*Dead?* Annabella? How can that be?" Kira was stunned. She had seen the old woman two days before. They had sipped tea together.

Matt took her question seriously. "It be like this," he replied. He flung himself to the ground, lay on his back with both arms outstretched, opened his eyes wide, and stared blankly upward. Branch, curious, nosed at his neck, but Matt held the pose.

Kira stared in dismay at his grotesque but accurate imitation of death. "Don't, Matt," she said at last. "Get up. Don't do that."

Matt sat up and took the dog into his lap. He tilted his head and looked at Kira curiously. "Probably they be giving you her stuff," he announced.

"You're certain it was Annabella?"

Matt nodded. "I seen her face when they tooken her to the Field." Briefly he made the death face again, with its blank eyes.

Kira bit her lip. She turned away from the path. Matt was correct, she should not go into the woods now. But she did not know where to go. She could wake Thomas, she supposed. But for what? Thomas had never met the old dyer.

Finally she turned and looked back at the large Council Edifice where she lived. The door through which she came and went was in the side wing. The large door in front was the one she had entered on the day of her trial so many weeks before. The Council of Guardians would probably not be meeting today in the big chamber where her trial had been. But Jamison must be someplace inside. She decided that she would look for him. He would know what had happened, would tell her what to do.

"No, Matt," she said when the tyke began to follow her.

His face fell. He had sensed an adventure. "Go wake Thomas," Kira told him. "Tell him what happened. Tell him that Annabella has died, and that I have gone to find Jamison."

"Jamison? Who's he?"

Kira was startled at Matt's ignorance. Jamison had become so much a part of her life that she had forgotten the tyke wouldn't know his name. "He's the guardian who first took me to my room," she explained. "Remember? A very tall man with dark hair? You were with us that day.

"He always wears one of Thomas's carvings," she added. "Quite a nice one, with an outline of a tree."

Matt nodded at that. "I seen him!" he said eagerly.

134

"Where?" Kira looked around. If Jamison was nearby, if she could find him at one of the workplaces, she wouldn't have to search the Council Edifice.

"He be there, watching, walking beside, when the draggers tooken the old dyer to the Field," Matt said.

So Jamison already knew.

The corridors were, as always, quiet and dim. At first Kira felt secretive and stealthy, as if she should make her footsteps as silent as possible, difficult with her stick and her dragging leg. Then she reminded herself that she was not hiding, not in danger. She was simply looking for the man who had been her mentor since her mother's death. She could even, if she chose, call his name loudly in hopes that he would hear and respond. But calling out seemed inappropriate and so she simply continued down the hall in silence.

As she had expected, the great hall was empty. She knew that it was used only for special occasions: the annual Gathering; trials, such as her own; and other ceremonies that she had never seen. She pulled the huge door open a crack, peeked in, and turned away to look elsewhere in the building.

She knocked timidly on several doors. Finally at one a voice answered with a gruff "Yes?" and she pushed the door open to see one of the tenders, a man she didn't recognize, busy at a desk.

"I'm looking for Jamison," Kira explained.

The tender shrugged. "He's not here."

She could see that. "Do you know where he might be?" she asked politely.

"In the wing, probably." The tender looked down again at his work. He seemed to be sorting papers.

Kira knew that "the wing" was where her own quarters were. That made sense. Probably Jamison was looking for her even now, to tell her of the old woman's death. She had started out much earlier than usual this morning, thinking to make up for the day wasted yesterday by rain. If she had waited, Jamison could have found her, told her of the death, explained, and she would not feel so shocked and solitary.

"Excuse me, but can I get to the wing from here without going back outside?"

Impatiently the tender gestured to his left. "Door at the end," he said.

Kira thanked him, closed his office door behind her, and went to the end of the long hall. The door there was not locked, and when she opened it she saw a familiar stairway. She had tiptoed down it with Thomas and Matt just yesterday during the storm. She knew the stairs would return her to the corridor above, where she would find her room and Thomas's.

She stood motionless and listened. The tender had said that Jamison was probably somewhere in the wing, but she heard no sound.

On a whim, instead of taking the stairs to her room, Kira remained on the first floor. She went to the corner where she and Thomas had hidden the day before, the same corner they had peered around to see where the crying was coming from. In the silence and emptiness, she rounded the corner and approached the door that had been open the afternoon before.

She leaned next to it, her ear against the wood, and listened. But there was no sound of crying, none of singing.

After a moment, she tried the knob. But the door was locked. Finally, very softly, she knocked.

She heard a rustling sound inside, then the muffled sound of small footsteps on a bare floor.

She knocked softly again.

She heard a whimper.

Kira knelt by the door. It was difficult, with her crippled leg. But she lowered herself until her mouth was beside the large keyhole. Then she called softly, "Jo?"

"I'm being good," a frightened, desperate little voice replied. "I'm practicing."

"I know you are," Kira said through the keyhole. She could hear small, shuddering sobs.

"I'm your friend, Jo. My name is Kira."

"Please, I want me mum," the tyke pleaded. She sounded very young.

For some reason Kira thought of the enclosure that had been built on the site of her old cott. Now tykes were penned there, enclosed by thorn bushes. It seemed cruel. But at least they were not isolated.

They had each other, and they were able to look out through the thick foliage and see the village life around them.

Why was this small tyke locked in a room all alone?

"I will come back," she called softly through the door.

"Will you bring me mum?" The little voice was close to the keyhole. Kira could almost feel the breath.

Matt had told her that the tyke's parents were both dead. "I will come back," Kira said again. "Jo? Listen to me."

The tyke sniffled. In the distance, on the floor above, Kira heard a door open.

"I must go," Kira whispered firmly through the hole. "But listen, Jo: I will help you, I promise. Hush now. Don't tell anyone I was here."

She rose quickly. Clutching her stick, she made her way back to the staircase. When she reached the second floor and rounded the corner, she saw Jamison standing in the open doorway to her room. He came forward, greeted her with sympathy, and told her the news of Annabella's death.

Suddenly wary, Kira said nothing of the child below.

15

"Look! They're setting up a dyeing-place for me."

It was midday. Kira pointed down to the area below the window, a small piece of land between the Edifice and the edge of the woods. Thomas came to the window and looked. Workers had raised a structure that Kira could see was to be a shed; under its roof, long poles from which to hang the wet yarns and threads to dry were already in place.

"It's better than anything she ever had," Kira murmured, remembering Annabella wistfully. "I'm going to miss her," she added.

It had all happened so quickly. Annabella's death, so sudden; and now, only a day later, the new dyeing-place was being made.

"What's that?" Thomas pointed. To the side, the workers were digging a shallow pit. A support for hanging kettles was being pounded into place at the side.

"It'll be for fire. You need a very hot fire always, for the boiling of the dyes.

"Oh, Thomas," Kira sighed, turning away from the window, "I'll never remember how to do it all."

"Yes you will. I have it all written down, everything you told me. We'll just repeat it and repeat it. Look! What's that they're bringing?"

She looked again and saw them stacking bundles of dried plants beside the new shed. "They must have brought all the ones Annabella had hanging from the beams in her cott. So at least I'll have a place to start. I think I know the names, if they haven't mixed them all together out of ignorance."

Then she chuckled, watching one of the workers set down a covered pot and turn his face away with a grimace of disgust. "It's the mordant," Kira explained. "It smells terrible." She didn't want to say the rude word to Thomas, but it was what Annabella had called her pisspot, and its contents were a surprisingly vital ingredient in the making of the dyes.

The workers had begun to arrive early that morning, bearing the kettles and plants and equipment, while Jamison was still in Kira's room describing the events of the day before. A sudden death, he had explained, the way death often came to those of great age. She slept, Annabella had, napping on the rainy day, and didn't wake. That was all. No mystery to it.

Perhaps she felt that she had completed her job by teaching Kira, Jamison pointed out solemnly. Sometimes, he told her, it was the way death came: a drifting-away when one's tasks were accomplished. "And there's no need to burn her cott," he added, "because there was no illness. So it will stay as it is. Someday you can live there, if you like, after you've finished your work here."

Kira nodded, accepting his words. The old woman's spirit, she realized, would still be in her body. "She'll need a watcher," Kira pointed out to Jamison. "Could I go and sit with her? I did for my mother."

But Jamison said no. Time was short. The Gathering was coming. Four days could not be lost. Kira must work on the robe; others would do the watching for the old dyer.

So Kira would mourn all alone.

After Jamison had gone she sat silently, remembering how solitary Annabella's chosen life had been, how unconnected to the village. Only then did it occur to Kira to wonder, *Who found her? How did they know to look?*

"Thomas, come away from the window now. I need to tell you about something."

Reluctantly he came to where she was sitting at the table, though she could see from his face that he was still listening to the noise of the construction below. *Boys,* Kira thought. They were always interested in such things. If Matt were around, he'd be down there underfoot, getting in the way, wanting to help with the building.

"This morning —" she began. Then, sensing his inattention, "Thomas! *Listen!*"

He grinned, turned toward her, and listened.

"I went to the room below, the one where we

141

heard the tyke crying."

"And singing," Thomas reminded her.

"Yes. And singing."

"Her name is Jo, according to Matt," Thomas said. "See? I'm paying attention. Why did you go down there?"

"I was looking for Jamison at first," Kira explained, "and I found myself on that floor. So I went to the door, thinking I might peek in and see if the tyke was all right. But it was locked!"

Thomas nodded. He looked unsurprised.

"But they've never locked *my* door, Thomas," she said.

"No, because you were already grown, already two syllables when you came here. But I was young; I was still Tom when I arrived," he said. "They locked my door."

"You were held *captive?*"

He frowned, remembering. "Not really. It was to keep me safe, I think. And to make me pay attention. I was young and I didn't want to work all the time." He grinned. "I was a little like Matt, I think. Playful."

"Were they harsh with you?" Kira asked, remembering the sound of Jamison's voice speaking to the little girl.

He thought. "Stern," he said finally.

"But, Thomas, the tyke below — Jo? She was crying. *Sobbing.* She wanted her mum, she said."

"Matt told us her mother died."

"She doesn't seem to know that."

Matt tried to recall his own circumstances. "I think they told me about my parents. But maybe not right away. It was a long time ago. I remember someone brought me here and showed me where everything was, and how it worked —"

"The bathroom and the hot water," Kira said, with a wry smile.

"Yes, that. And all the tools. I was already a Carver. I'd been carving for a long time —"

"— the way I'd already been doing the threadings. And the way the tyke, Jo —"

"Yes," Thomas said. "Matt said she was already a singer."

Kira, thinking, smoothed the folds of her skirt. "So each of us," she said slowly, "was already a — I don't know what to call it."

"Artist?" Thomas suggested. "That's a word. I've never heard anyone say it, but I've read it in some of the books. It means, well, someone who is able to make something beautiful. Would that be the word?"

"Yes, I guess it would. The tyke makes her singing, and it is beautiful."

"When she isn't crying," Thomas pointed out.

"So we are each artists, and we were each orphaned, and they brought us each here. I wonder why. Also, Thomas, there's something else. Something strange."

He was listening.

"This morning I talked to Marlena, a woman I

know from the weaving shed. She lives in the Fen, and she remembered Jo, though she didn't know her name. She remembered a singing tyke."

"Everyone in the Fen would know of such a tyke."

Kira nodded, agreeing. "She said — how did she put it?" She tried to remember Marlena's description. "She said that the tyke seemed to have knowledges."

"Knowledges?"

"That was the word she used."

"What did she mean?"

"She said that the tyke seemed to have knowledge of things that hadn't happened yet. That the people in the Fen thought it was magic. She sounded a little frightened when she talked of it. And, Thomas?"

"What?" he asked.

Kira hesitated. "It made me think of what happens sometimes with my cloth. This small one." Kira opened the box he had made for her and held out the fabric scrap, reminding him. "I told you how it seems to speak to me.

"And I remember that you told me that you have a piece of wood that seems to do the same —"

"Yes. From when I was just a tyke, just beginning to carve. The one on the shelf. I've shown it to you."

"Could it be the same thing?" Kira asked cautiously. "Could it be what Marlena called *knowledges?*"

Thomas looked at her, and at the cloth that lay

motionless in her hand. He frowned. "But why?" he asked at last.

Kira didn't know the answer. "Maybe it is something that artists have," she said, liking the sound of the word she had just learned. "A special kind of magic knowledge."

Thomas nodded and shrugged. "Well, it doesn't matter much, does it? We each have a good life now. Better tools than we did before. Good food. Work to do."

"But the tyke below? She sobs and sobs. And they won't let her out of the room." Kira remembered her promise. "Thomas, I told her I'd come back. And that I'd help her."

He looked dubious. "I don't think the guardians would like that."

Kira again remembered the severity she had heard in Jamison's voice. She remembered the slamming of the door. "No, I don't think they would," she agreed. "But at night. I'll creep down then, when they think we're all asleep. Except —" Her face fell.

"Except what?"

"It's locked. There's no way I can get in."

"Yes you can," Thomas told her.

"How?"

"I have a key," he said.

It was true. Back in his room, he showed her. "It was a long time ago," he explained. "But here I was, locked in, with all these fine tools. So I carved a key. It really was quite easy. The lock on the door is a simple one.

"And," he added, fingering the intricately carved wooden key, "it fits all the doors. All the locks are the same. I know because I tried them. I used to go out at night and roam the hallways, opening doors. All the rooms were empty then."

Kira shook her head. "You were really mischievous, weren't you?"

Thomas grinned. "I told you. Just like Matt."

"Tonight," Kira said, suddenly serious. "Will you come with me?"

Thomas nodded. "All right," he agreed. "Tonight."

16

Evening came. Kira, in Thomas's room, looked down through the window at the squalor of the village and listened to its chaotic din as workers in the various sheds finished their last chores. Down the lane she could see how the butcher threw a container of water over the stone doorstep of his hut, a useless gesture toward cleaning away the clotted filth. Nearer, she watched the women leaving the weaving shed where she had worked as helper for so much of her childhood.

Kira wondered, smiling, whether Matt had been there during the workday that had just ended. Assigned to cleaning-up chores, he had probably been underfoot with his mates, making trouble and stealing food from the women's lunches. From her place at the window, she couldn't see any sign of him or of his dog. She hadn't seen them all day.

She waited there with Thomas until long past dark, until the tenders had taken their food trays away. At last the entire building was still and the clamor from the village had subsided as well.

"Thomas," Kira suggested, "take your little piece

of wood. The special one. I have my scrap with me."

"All right, but why?"

"I don't know exactly. I feel that we should."

Thomas got the small carved piece from its high shelf, and put it into his pocket. In his other pocket was the wooden key.

Together they went down the dimly lit corridor to the stairs.

Ahead of her, Thomas whispered, "Shhhh."

"I'm sorry," Kira whispered back. "The stick makes a noise. But I can't walk without it."

"Here, wait." They stopped beside one of the wall torches. Thomas ripped a length of cloth from the hem of his loose shirt. Deftly he tied it around the base of Kira's walking stick. The cloth muted the noise of the wooden stick on the tiled floor.

The pair made their way quickly down the flight of stairs and to the door of the room where Jo slept. They paused there and listened. But there were no sounds. Kira's hand, in her pocket, felt no warning from her scrap of cloth. She nodded to Thomas and silently he inserted the big key and turned it to open the door.

Kira held her breath because she feared that a tender might be sharing the room to guard the tyke at night. But the room, illuminated only by pale moonlight through the window, held only one small bed and one small fast-asleep girl.

"I'll stay by the door to watch," Thomas murmured. "She knows you — or your voice, at least.

You wake her."

Kira went to the bed and sat on its edge, propping her stick beside her. Gently she touched the small shoulder. "Jo," she said softly.

The little head, long hair tangled, turned restlessly. After a moment, the tyke opened her eyes with a startled, frightened look. "No, don't!" she cried out, pushing Kira's hand away.

"Shhhh," Kira whispered. "It's me. Remember, we talked through the door? Don't be afraid."

"I want me mum," the tyke wailed.

She was very small. Much smaller than Matt. Hardly more than a toddler. Kira remembered the power of the singing voice that she had heard, and marveled that it had come from this tiny, frightened waif of a thing.

Kira picked her up, cradled her, and rocked her back and forth. "Shhhh," she said. "Shhhh. It's all right. I'm your friend. And see over there? His name is Thomas. He's your friend too."

Gradually the tyke was soothed. Her eyes opened wide. Her thumb slid into her mouth and she spoke around it. "I be listening to you at the hole," she said, remembering.

"Yes, the keyhole. We whispered to each other."

"You know me mum? Can you bring her?"

Kira shook her head. "No, I'm afraid I can't. But I'll be here. I live just upstairs. And Thomas does, too."

Thomas came nearer and knelt by the bed. The

tyke stared at him suspiciously, and clutched Kira.

Thomas pointed to the ceiling. "I live right above you," he said in a gentle voice, "and I can hear you."

"You hear me singings?"

He smiled. "Yes. Your singing is very beautiful."

The tyke scowled. "They always be making me learn new ones."

"New songs?" Kira asked her.

Jo nodded unhappily. "Over and over. They be making me remember everythings. Me old songs, they just be there natural. But now they be stuffing new things into me and this poor head hurts horrid." The tyke rubbed her tangled hair and sighed, a strangely adult sound that made Kira smile sympathetically.

Thomas was looking around the room, which held many of the same pieces of furniture as the rooms above. A bed. A tall wooden chest of drawers. A table and two chairs.

"Jo," he said suddenly, "are you a good climber?"

She frowned and removed her thumb from her mouth. "I be climbing trees sometimes in the Fen. But me mum, she hits me when I do because she say I be breaking me legs and then they take me to the Field."

Thomas nodded solemnly. "Yes, that's probably true, and your mother didn't want you to get hurt."

"Once draggers take you to the Field, you don't never come back. Beasts take you." The thumb popped back in.

"But look, Jo. If you could climb up there —"
Thomas pointed to the top of the chest of drawers.

The wide eyes followed his pointing finger, and
the tyke nodded.

"If you stood very tall up there, and if you had
some tool, you could hit the ceiling and I would hear
you."

The tyke grinned at the thought. "You mustn't do
it just for fun," Thomas added quickly. "Only if you
really needed us."

"Might I be trying it?" Jo asked eagerly.

Kira lifted her down to the floor. Like a limber
animal the tyke scrambled from chair to tabletop,
and from the tabletop she climbed to the top of the
chest. Then she stood triumphantly. From below her
woven nightdress emerged two bare thin legs.

"We need a tool," Thomas murmured, looking
around.

Remembering something from her own quarters,
Kira went to the bathroom. As she had guessed, a
thick hairbrush with a wooden handle lay on the
shelf beside the sink.

"Try this," she said, and handed it up to the tyke.

Smiling broadly, the little singer reached up and
thumped the brush handle on the ceiling.

Thomas lifted her down and put her back into the
bed. "That's it, then," he said. "If you need us, that's
the signal, Jo. But never just for fun. Only if you need
help."

"And we'll come to see you too, even if you don't thump," Kira added. "After the tenders are gone." She tucked the bed covers around the tyke. "Here, Thomas. Put this back, would you?" She handed him the hairbrush.

"We must go now," she told Jo. "But do you feel better, knowing that you have friends up there?"

The tyke nodded. Her moist thumb slid into her mouth.

Kira smoothed the blanket. "Good night, then." For a moment she sat there on the bed, feeling a vague memory of something else that should be done. Something from when she was a small tyke, like this, being put to bed.

She leaned down toward the little girl, intuitively. What was it that her mother had done when she was small? Kira put her lips on Jo's forehead. It was an unfamiliar gesture but felt right.

The little girl made a small contented sound with her own lips against Kira's face. "A little kissie," she whispered. "Like me mum."

Kira and Thomas parted in the upstairs corridor and made their way separately back to their own rooms. It was late, and as always they were expected to work in the morning and needed sleep.

As Kira prepared for bed, she thought about the frightened, lonely tyke below. What songs were they forcing her to learn? Why was she here at all?

Ordinarily an orphaned tyke would be turned over to another family.

It was the same question that she and Thomas had discussed the day before. And the answer seemed to be the conclusion they had reached: they were artists, the three of them. Makers of song, of wood, of threaded patterns. Because they were artists, they had some value that she could not comprehend. Because of that value, the three of them were here, well fed, well housed, and nurtured.

She brushed her hair and teeth and got into bed. The window was open to the breeze. Below, she could see the half-completed constructions that would soon be her dyeing-garden, firepit, and shed. Across the room, through the darkness, she could see the folded, covered shape on top of her worktable: the Singer's robe.

Suddenly Kira knew that although her door was unlocked, she was not really free. Her life was limited to these things and this work. She was losing the joy she had once felt when the bright-colored threads took shape in her hands, when the patterns came to her and were her own. The robe did not belong to her, though she was learning its story through her work. She would almost be able to tell the history now that it had passed through her fingers, now that she had focused on it so closely for so many days. But it was not what her hands or heart yearned to do.

Thomas, uncomplaining though he was, had

mentioned the headaches that afflicted him after hours of work. So had the little singer below. *They be stuffing new things into me,* the tyke had whimpered. She wanted the freedom to sing her own songs as she always had.

Kira did too. She wanted her hands to be free of the robe so that they could make patterns of their own again. Suddenly she wished that she could leave this place, despite its comforts, and return to the life she had known.

She buried her face in the bedclothes and for the first time cried in despair.

17

"Thomas, I've worked hard all morning, and you have too. Would you take a walk with me? There's something I want to see."

It was midday. They had both eaten lunch.

"You want to go down and look at what the workmen are doing? I'll go with you." Thomas set aside the carving tool he had just picked up. Kira noticed again, with admiration, how intricate the work was on the large Singer's staff. Thomas had been smoothing the tiny rough spots from the worn, ancient carvings and reshaping the infinitesimally small edges and curves. It was very similar to the work that Kira herself had been assigned, the repair of the Singer's robe. And the entire top of the staff was undecorated; it was smooth, uncarved wood, in the same way that the expanse across the shoulders of the robe was untouched cloth. Kira's work was approaching that unadorned expanse. So was Thomas's, she realized.

"What will you carve there?" she asked him, pointing to the undecorated part.

"I don't know. They said they'd tell me."

She watched as he carefully laid the staff across the table.

"Actually," she told him, "if you want to look at what the workmen are doing, I'll go there with you later. But that's not what I had in mind. Will you go with me first where *I* want?"

Thomas nodded good-naturedly. "Where's that?" he asked.

"The Fen," Kira told him.

He looked at her quizzically. "That filthy place? Why would you want to go there?"

"I've never been there. I want to see where Jo lived, Thomas."

"And Matt does still," he reminded her.

"Yes, Matt too. I wonder where he is, Thomas." Kira was uneasy. "I haven't seen him in two days. Have you?"

Thomas shook his head. "Maybe he found another source of food," he suggested, laughing.

"Matt could point out where Jo lived. Maybe I could even bring something back for her. Maybe she had toys. Did they let you bring things when you came here, Thomas?"

He shook his head. "Just my bits of wood. They didn't want me distracted."

Kira sighed. "She's so small. She should have a toy. Maybe you could carve her a doll? And I could stitch a little dress for it."

"I could, I guess," Thomas agreed. He handed Kira her walking stick. "Let's go," he said. "We'll probably find Matt along the way. Or he'll find us."

Together the pair made their way out of the Edifice, across the plaza, and down the crowded lane. At the weaving shed, Kira paused, greeted the women, and asked about Matt.

"Haven't seen him! And good riddance, too!" one of the workers replied. "The useless scamp!"

"When're you coming back, Kira?" another asked. "We could use your help. And you're old enough to be on the looms now! With your mother gone, you must need the work!"

But another woman laughed loudly and pointed to Kira's clean new clothes. "She don't need us no more!"

The looms began to click and move again. Kira turned away.

Nearby, she heard an oddly familiar, oddly frightening sound. A low growl. Quickly she glanced around, half expecting to see a menacing dog or something worse. But the sound had come from a cluster of women near the butcher's. They burst into laughter when they saw her looking. She saw Vandara in their midst. The scarred woman turned her back on Kira and she heard the growl again: a human imitation of a beast. Kira lowered her head and limped past them, ignoring the cruel laughter.

Thomas had gone ahead; she could see him far beyond the butcher's. He had stopped near a group of young boys playing in the mud.

"Dunno!" one was saying as she approached.

"Gimme coins and maybe I could find him!"

"I asked them about Matt," Thomas explained, "but they say they haven't seen him."

"Do you suppose he might be sick?" Kira asked, worried. "His nose is always running. Maybe we should never have cleaned him up. He was accustomed to that layer of dirt."

The boys, slapping their bare feet in the mud, were listening. "Matt's the strongest of the strong!" one said. "He never be sick!"

A smaller one wiped his own runny nose on the back of his hand. "His mum be yelling at him. I heared her. And she throwed a rock at him too, and he laughed at it and run off!"

"When?" Kira asked the runny-nosed boy.

"Dunno," he said. "Maybe two days ago."

"It were!" chimed in another. "Two days ago! I seed it too. His mum chucked a rock at him 'cause he tooken some food! He said he were goin' on a journey!"

"He's all right, Kira," Thomas reassured her, and they walked on. "He takes care of himself better than most adults. Here — I think this is where we turn."

She followed him down an unfamiliar narrow lane. The huts were closer together here, and close to the edge of the woods, so that they were shaded by trees and smelled of dankness and rot. They came to a foul-smelling stream and crossed it by a slippery, primitive bridge of logs. Thomas took her hand and helped her; it was treacherous, with her bad leg, and she feared slipping into the water, which was quite shallow but clogged with filth.

On the other side of the stream, beyond the thick poisonous oleander bushes that were such a danger to tykes, lay the area known as the Fen. In some ways it was similar to the place that Kira had called home: the small cotts, close together; the incessant wailing of infants; the stench of smoky fires, rotting food, and unwashed humans. But it was darker here, with the trees thick overhead, and festering with dampness and an odor of ill health.

"Why must there be such a horrible place?" Kira whispered to Thomas. "Why do people have to live like this?"

"It's how it is," he replied, frowning. "It's always been."

A sudden vision slid into Kira's mind. The robe. The robe told how it had always been; and what Thomas had said was not true. There had been times — oh, such long ago times — when people's lives had been golden and green. Why could there not be such times again? She began to say it to him.

"Thomas," she suggested, "you and I? We're the ones who will fill in the blank places. Maybe we can make it different."

But she saw how he was looking at her. His look was skeptical, amused.

"What are you talking about?" He didn't understand. Perhaps he never would.

"Nothing," Kira told him, shaking her head.

As they walked, an ominous quiet fell. Kira became aware of eyes. Women stood in shadowed doorways, watching them suspiciously. Kira limped along, trying to find ways around the garbage-strewn puddles in the path, and felt the hostile stares. It made no sense, she knew, to walk without a destination through this unfamiliar, malevolent place.

"Thomas," she murmured, "we must ask someone."

He stopped, and she stopped beside him. They stood uncertainly in the path.

"What be your purpose?" a hoarse voice called from an open window. Kira looked, and saw a green lizard slither into the vines at the sill; behind the fluttering wet leaves a gaunt-faced woman was holding a tyke in her arms and looking out. There seemed no men around. She realized the men, mostly draggers and diggers, would all be working, and she felt relieved, remembering how they had grabbed at her the day of the weapons.

Kira made her way through the thorny underbrush and went closer to the window. Through it, she could see the dark interior of the cott, where several other tykes, half-naked, stood staring dull-eyed and frightened toward her.

"I'm looking for the boy called Matt," she said politely to the woman. "Do you know where he lives?"

"What you be giving me fer it?"

"Giving you? I'm sorry," Kira told her, startled by

the question. "I don't have anything to give."

"Nary food?"

"No. I'm sorry." Kira held her hands out, show-ing that they were empty.

"I have an apple." Thomas approached and to Kira's surprise, took a dark red apple from his pock-et. "I saved it from lunch," he explained to Kira in a low voice, and he held it toward the woman.

Her thin arm reached out from the open window and grabbed the fruit. She bit at it and began to turn away.

"Wait!" Kira said. "The cott where Matt lives! Can you tell us, please?"

The woman turned back, her mouth full. "Further down," she said, chewing noisily. The infant in her arms grabbed at the bitten apple, and she shoved its hands away. She gestured with her head. "There be a busted tree in front."

Kira nodded. "And please, one more thing," she pleaded. "What can you tell us about a tyke named Jo?"

The woman's face changed and Kira found it hard to interpret the look. For a moment, a brief flicker of joy had washed across the thin, embittered face. Then hopelessness replaced it.

"The little singing girl," the woman said, her voice a hoarse whisper. "She be tooken. They tooken her away."

She turned away abruptly and disappeared into the shadowed interior of the cott. Her children began to cry and to claw at her for food.

The gnarled tree was dying, split almost to the ground and rotting. Perhaps it had once borne fruit. But now its limbs were broken, dangling at odd angles, punctuated by occasional wisps of brown leaves.

The small cott behind the tree looked damaged and neglected too. But there were voices inside: a woman speaking roughly and a sharp-tongued child answering her in an angry, spiteful tone.

Thomas knocked. The voices became quiet and finally the door opened slightly.

"Who you be?" the woman asked abruptly.

"We're friends of Matt's," Thomas told her. "Is he inside? Is he all right?"

"Who be it, Mum?" the child's voice called.

The woman peered at Thomas and Kira silently, not answering. Finally Thomas called to the child, "Is Matt at home?"

"What's he done now? What you be wanting him for?" the woman asked, her eyes glinting with mistrust.

"He runned off! And tooken food too!" A tyke called to them; his head, thick with tousled, unkempt hair, appeared beside the woman. He pushed the door open wider.

Kira looked in dismay at the cott's dark interior. A pitcher, overturned on a table, lay in a puddle of some thick liquid through which insects crawled. The tyke at the door picked his nose with one finger, scratched himself with the other hand, and stared at them. His mother coughed wetly and then spat something to the floor.

"Do you know where he went?" Kira asked, trying not to show how shocked she felt at the condition of these people.

The woman shook her head and coughed again. "Good rid to him," she said. She shoved the tyke to the side and pulled the heavy wooden door closed.

After a moment, Kira and Matt turned away. Behind them, they heard the door open. "Miss? I know where Matt goed," the tyke's voice said. He emerged from the cott despite his mother's scolding voice and came to them. He was clearly Matt's brother. He had the same bright, mischievous eyes.

They waited.

"What you gimme?" His finger went into his nose again.

Kira sighed. Life in the Fen was apparently a series of barters. No wonder Matt had become such a clever manipulator and entrepreneur. She looked helplessly at Thomas.

"We don't have anything to give you," she explained to the tyke.

He eyed her appraisingly. "How about that there, miss?" he suggested, pointing to Kira's neck. She touched the thong from which hung the polished stone.

"No," she told the tyke, and her fingers curled

protectively around the stone. "This was my mother's. I can't give it to you."

To her surprise, he nodded as if that made sense to him. "That there, then?" He pointed to her hair. Kira remembered that she had tied it back that morning, as she often did, with a simple leather cord of no value. Quickly she pulled it loose and held it out.

The tyke grabbed it and thrust it into his pocket. It seemed to be a satisfactory payment. "Our mum, she thrashed Matt so hard he was horrid bloody, and so him and Branchie, they goed on a journey and they not be coming back, not to the Fen," the tyke announced. "Matt, he got friends who be taking good care of him, not thrashing him *never!* And they give him food, too."

Thomas laughed a little. "And they make him take baths," he added, though the tyke just stared, not understanding the word.

"But he meant us!" Kira pointed out. "*We're* the friends he meant!" She was concerned. "If he tried to come to us, where is he? It was two days ago that he left here, and no one's seen him since. He knew the way to —"

Matt's brother interrupted her. "Him and Branchie, they goed someplace else first. He be getting a giftie for his friends. That be you, miss? And you?" He looked at Thomas.

They nodded.

"Matt, he say that a giftie makes a person like you best of all."

164

Kira sighed in exasperation. "No, that's not the way it is. A gift —" She gave up. "Never mind. Tell us where he went."

"He be getting you some *blue!*"

"Blue? What do you mean?"

"Dunno, miss. But Matt, he said it. He be saying they got blue yonder, and he be getting you some."

The woman reappeared in the open doorway and called in a shrill and angry voice to the tyke, who retreated inside. Thomas and Kira turned away and began to retrace their steps on the muddy path back toward the village. Silent watchers still lurked in doorways. The fetid air still hung humid.

Kira whispered to Thomas. "When Matt disappeared, I thought perhaps we would find that he had been taken too. Like Jo."

"If he'd been taken," Thomas suggested, "we'd know his whereabouts. He'd be there with us in the Council Edifice."

Kira nodded. "And with Jo. Although maybe they'd have locked him up, like her. He'd hate that."

"Matt would find a way to get free," Thomas pointed out. "Anyway," he added, helping Kira find her way around a puddle with a dead rat in it, "they wouldn't want Matt, I'm afraid. They only want us for our skills, and he hasn't any."

Kira thought of the impish boy, of his generosity and his laughter, of his devotion to the little dog. She thought of him now, wherever he was, on his quest to bring a gift to friends. "Oh, Thomas," she said, "he *does*. He knows just how to make us smile and laugh."

There seemed no hint of laughter or any history of it in this terrible place. Making her way through the squalor, Kira remembered Matt's infectious chortle. She thought, too, of the clear purity of the small singer's voice, and how the two children must have been the only elements of joy here. Now Jo had been taken away. And Matt was gone as well.

She wondered where he could have journeyed, all alone but for the dog, to search for blue.

18

The day of the Gathering was approaching. Its near-
ness was palpable in the village. People began to finish projects and delayed the start of new ones. Kira
noticed that in the weaving shed fabrics were folded
and stacked, but the looms were not restrung.

The noise level subsided, as if people were distracted with preparations and didn't want to waste
time with the usual bickering.

Some people washed.

In his room, Thomas was meticulously polishing
the Singer's staff again and again. He used thick oils
and rubbed them into the wood with a soft cloth.
Smooth and golden, it began to take on a glow and
fragrance.

Matt did not return. It had been many days now
since he had disappeared. At night, before she slept,
Kira held the scrap of cloth that had so often
assuaged her fears and even answered her questions.
She wrapped it around her fingers and concentrated
on Matt; she pictured the laughing boy and sought
some feeling of where he might be and whether he
was safe. A feeling of reassurance, of solace, came

from the scrap. But no answer.

They could occasionally hear the voice of the small singer, Jo, during the day. The crying had ceased. Most often they heard repetitive chanting, the same phrases over and over, though sometimes, as if she were allowed a moment of her own, the high lyrical voice soared into melodies that made Kira hold her breath in awe.

She crept down at night with the key in her hand and visited the tyke. Jo had stopped asking for her mother, but she clung to Kira in the darkness. Together they whispered little stories and jokes. Kira brushed Jo's hair.

"I could thump with the hairbrush iffen I needed," Jo reminded her, looking up at the ceiling.

"Yes. And we would come." Kira stroked Jo's soft cheek.

"Want I should make a song for you?" Jo asked.

"Someday," Kira told her. "But not now. We mustn't make noise in the night. It must be our secret, that I come here."

"I be thinking up a song," Jo said. "And someday I sing it for you horrid loud."

"All right." Kira laughed.

"The Gathering be soon," Jo said importantly.

"Yes, I know."

"I be right up front, they say."

"Good for you! So you'll be able to see everything. You'll be able to see the beautiful Singer's robe. I've been working on it," Kira told her. "It has wonderful colors."

"When I be Singer," the tyke confided, "then I can make my own songs again. Iffen I learn the old ones good."

When Jamison came to her room, Kira showed him that the repairs to the robe were complete. He was obviously pleased with her work. Together they spread the fabric across the table, turning it, unfolding its pleating and cuffs, examining the intricate stitches and the scenes they created.

"You've done a fine job, Kira," he said. "Particularly here."

He pointed to a place that she recalled had been difficult for her; though tiny in size, as each embroidered scene was, it was a complicated portrayal of tall buildings in shades of gray, each of them toppling, against a background of fiery explosions. Kira had matched oranges and reds of different shades and had found the various grays for the smoke and the buildings. But the threading had been hard for her because she had no sense of what the buildings were. She had never seen anything like them. The Council Edifice in which she lived and worked was the only large building she knew, and it was small compared to these. These, before they toppled, had seemed to extend up into the sky to amazing heights, much, much higher than any tree she had ever seen.

"That was the hardest part," she told Jamison. "It was so complicated. Perhaps if I had known more about the buildings, about what happened to them —"

She was embarrassed. "I should have paid more attention to the Ruin Song each year," she confessed. "I was always so excited when it began, but then my mind would wander a bit, and I didn't always listen carefully."

"You were young," Jamison reminded her, "and the Song is very, very long. No one listens carefully to every part, and especially not the tykes."

"This year I will!" Kira told him. "This year I'll be paying special attention because I know the scenes so well. I'll be listening especially for this scene, with the buildings falling."

Jamison closed his eyes. She could see his lips move silently. He started to hum, and she recognized a recurrent melody from part of the Song. Then he began to chant aloud:

Burn, scourged world,
Furious furnace,
Inferno impure —

He opened his eyes. "I believe that's the part," he said. "It goes on and on after that — I forget the next words - but I believe that's the part where the buildings toppled. Of course I've listened to the Song for many more years than you."

"I can't imagine how the Singer remembers it all," Kira said. For a moment she thought of asking him about the captive child below, the Singer of the future, who was being forced to learn the interminable Song. But she hesitated, and the moment passed.

"Of course he has the staff as a guide," Jamison said. "And he began the learning when he was just a small tyke. That was a very long time ago. And he rehearses constantly. While you've been preparing his robe, he's been preparing this year's Song. The words are always the same, of course, but I believe he decides, each year, to emphasize certain parts. He studies all year, planning and rehearsing the singing of it."

"Where?"

"He has special quarters in a different section of the Edifice."

"I've never seen him except at the time of the Song."

"No. He stays apart."

They turned again to the robe, examining each section to be certain that Kira had missed nothing. A tender brought tea and they sat together, talking of the robe and its stories, of the history it told, of the time before the Ruin. Jamison closed his eyes again and recited.

> Ravaged all,
> Bogo tabal
> Timore toron
> Totoo now gone...

Kira recognized the lines, some of her favorites, though she didn't understand them. As a tyke the rhyming sounds had charmed her out of the boredom she often felt during the interminable Song. "Bogo tabal, timore toron," she had chanted to herself at times.

"What does it mean, that section?" she asked Jamison now.

"I believe it tells the names of lost places," he explained.

"I wonder what those places looked like. *Timore toron.* I like the sounds."

"That's part of your job," Jamison reminded her. "You use the threads to remind us of how they looked."

Kira nodded and smoothed the robe again, finding the tragic toppling cities and the interspersed meadows of soft greens.

Jamison set his teacup on the table, went to the window, and looked down. "The workers are finished. After the Gathering and this year's Song, you'll be able to start dyeing new threads for the robe."

She looked up, dismayed, hoping to see by his expression that he was making a small joke. But his look was solemn. Kira had thought that when this work was complete she could turn to her own projects, to some of the elaborate patterns that she could feel and see in her mind. Sometimes her fingers quivered with the desire to make those scenes. "Will the robe become so damaged during the Song that it will need repairing again?" she asked him, trying not to show how distressing the thought was to her. She wanted to please him. He had been her protector. But she didn't want to keep doing this forever.

"No, no." His voice was reassuring. "Your mother kept up with the small repairs each year. And now you've very capably redone the places that needed restoration. After this year's Song there will probably be only a few scattered broken threads for you to fix."

"Then —?" Kira was puzzled.

Jamison reached toward the robe and gestured at the empty unadorned expanse across the shoulders. "Here lies the future," he said.

"And now you will tell it to us, with your fingers and your threads," he told her. His eyes had a piercing, excited look.

She tried to conceal her shock. "So soon?" she murmured. He had referred to this enormous task before. But she had thought that when she was older — when she had more skill — more knowledge —

"We have waited a long time for you," he said, and looked at her firmly as if he dared her to refuse.

19

It began early. At dawn Kira could hear the sounds, even from her room on the opposite side of the building, as the people started to gather. Quickly she finished dressing, pulled the brush through her hair, and ran to Thomas's room on the other side of the corridor. From there they could look down at the plaza where all large gatherings took place.

Unlike the day of the hunt, this crowd was subdued. Even small tykes, usually so unruly, clung to their mothers' hands and waited quietly. The sound that had awakened Kira was not shouts and jostling but simply the tread of feet as the people streamed up the narrow lanes and moved into the throng waiting to enter the building. From the Fen path came a steady flow of silent citizens clutching and leading their tykes. From the opposite direction, from the area where Kira and her mother had lived, came others whom she recognized from her old neighborhood. There was her mother's widowed brother with his boy, Dan, but the small girl, Mar, was not with him; perhaps she had been given away.

On a typical day, families were scattered and

apart, tykes scampering unsupervised, parents at work; but today hubbies stood with their wives and tykes with their families. The people seemed solemn and expectant.

"Where's the staff?" Kira asked, looking around Thomas's room.

"They took it yesterday."

Kira nodded. They had come and taken the robe yesterday as well. Weary though she was of the work, her room seemed diminished with it gone.

"Should we go down?" she asked him, though she didn't relish the prospect of joining the crowd.

"No, they said they'd come for us. I asked the tender who brought my breakfast.

"Look!" Thomas pointed. "Over there, way in the back. See, by the tree just before the weaving shed? Isn't that Matt's mother?"

Kira followed his pointing finger with her eyes and found the same gaunt woman who had eyed them suspiciously from the squalor of the cott. Today she was washed and tidy; beside her, holding her hand, was the tyke who looked so much like Matt. The two stood waiting as a family. But there was no second child. No Matt. A wave of sorrow swept through Kira, a feeling of loss.

Looking down at the sea of faces, Kira gradually recognized people here and there: the weaving women, separate from each other, each with a hubby and children; the butcher, clean for a change, with his large wife and two tall sons. The entire village had gathered now, only a few stragglers still hurrying up the lanes.

A small surge of movement began and she could see that the people were shuffling forward. The crowd rippled like water moving on the riverbank when a log floated by.

"The doors must have been opened," Thomas said, leaning forward to see.

They watched as the entire village, person by person, entered the building. Finally, when the crowd outside was almost entirely gone — and now they could hear the murmur of voices and the shuffle of footsteps from below, inside the building — a tender appeared in Thomas's doorway and beckoned.

"It's time," the tender said.

Except for a quick peek through a cracked-open door when she looked for Jamison one afternoon, Kira had not seen inside the Council of Guardians hall since the day of her trial months before. The circumstances had been so different then, when she entered the cavernous room and limped alone down its central aisle hungry, lonely, and fearful for her life.

Today she still leaned, as she had that day, on her stick. But now she was clean, healthy, and unafraid. Today she and Thomas were brought through a side entrance near the front, so that they saw the faces of the village watching them.

The tender pointed, directing them to a row of three wooden chairs on the left, just below the stage, facing the audience. Kira could see that there was another, longer row of chairs on the opposite side, and she recognized the Council of Guardians members who were already seated there. Jamison was among them.

Quickly, reminding herself of the custom, she bowed her head toward the Worship-object on the stage. Then she followed Thomas, and together they took their places in two of the chairs. A murmur passed through the audience and Kira felt her face flush in embarrassment. She didn't like being singled out. She didn't want to sit here at the front. She remembered the derisive voice of one of the weavers only a few days before. "She don't need us no more!" the woman had called.

It's not true. I need all of you. We need each other.

Gazing at the crowded audience, Kira remembered the many past years when she had come dutifully with her mother to the Gathering. Always they sat in the back where she couldn't see or hear, and she had endured the event bored and restless, sometimes kneeling on her seat to try to peer around the spectators' shoulders and get a glimpse of the Singer. Her mother, she remembered, had always been attentive and had gently restrained her when she wriggled in the seat. But the Gathering and the Song were long and difficult for tykes.

The people in the crowded audience, who though respectful had been shifting in their seats and whispering, quieted completely when Kira and Thomas entered and took their places. Everyone waited. Finally, in the silence, the four-syllable chief guardian, whom Kira had not seen since the trial and whose name she still could not recall (was it Bartholemew, perhaps?), rose from his seat on the other side. He walked to the space at the front of the stage and began the ritual that always opened the ceremony.

"The Gathering begins," he announced.

"We worship the Object," he said, gesturing toward the stage, and bowing. The entire audience bowed respectfully toward the little crossed construction of wood.

"I present the Council of Guardians," he said next, and nodded to the row of men which included Jamison. As a group, they stood. For a nervous moment Kira couldn't remember if the spectators were supposed to applaud. But a hush had fallen and the crowd was silent, though some heads seemed to nod toward the Council of Guardians in respect.

"For the first time I present the Carver of the future." He gestured toward Thomas, who looked uncertain.

"Stand," Kira whispered under her breath, knowing intuitively that it was the proper thing to do. Thomas stood awkwardly, shifting from one foot to the other. Again, heads nodded in respect. He sat back down.

She knew that she would be next, and she reached for her stick, which was leaning against the chair.

"For the first time I present the Robe-threader, the designer of the future."

Kira stood as straight as she could and acknowledged the nods in her direction. She sat again.

"For the first time, I present the Singer of the future. One day she will wear the robe."

The eyes of the villagers all turned to the side door, which had opened. Kira could see two tenders push Jo forward, pointing to the unoccupied chair. The tyke, dressed in a new but simple and unadorned gown, looked confused and uncertain, but her eyes found Kira's and Kira beckoned to her, smiling. Jo grinned and hurried forward toward the chair.

"Don't sit yet," Kira whispered. "Stand and look at the people. Be proud."

With a shy grin, with one foot nervously rubbing the ankle of the other leg, the Singer of the future stood and faced the crowd. Her smile, hesitant at first, quickly became both self-confident and infectious. Kira could see the people smile back.

"Now you can sit," Kira whispered.

"Wait," Jo whispered back. She raised one hand and waggled her fingers at the audience. A ripple of gentle laughter ran through the large crowd.

Then Jo turned and hoisted her small self, knees first, onto the chair. "I be giving them a little wavie," she confided to Kira.

"Finally, I present our Singer, who wears the robe," the chief guardian announced, when the people had quieted.

The Singer, wearing the magnificent robe and holding the carved staff in his right hand, entered from the other side. The crowd gasped collectively. Of course they saw him, and the robe, each year. But this year was different because of the work that Kira had done on the ancient embroidery. As the Singer moved toward the stage, the folds of the robe glistened in the torchlight; the colors of the threaded scenes glowed in their subtlety. Golds, light yellows deepening to vibrant orange, reds from the palest pink to the darkest crimson, greens, all shades, threaded in their intricate patterns, told the history of the world and its Ruin. As he turned to mount the few stairs to the stage, Kira could see the broad blank expanse across the Singer's back and shoulders, the blank that she had been picked to fill. The future that she had been chosen to create.

"What's that noise?" Thomas murmured.

Kira had been distracted by her awareness and appreciation of the robe and all that it meant. But now she heard it too: a dull, intermittent metallic noise, a muted clank. Now it was gone. There; she heard it again. A scraping clank.

"I don't know," she whispered back.

The Singer turned, at the center of the stage, after bowing slightly to the Worship-object, and now faced the audience. He fingered the staff like a talisman but did not need its guidance yet. His face was impassive, expressionless. Then he closed his eyes and began to breathe deeply.

The mysterious sound had disappeared. Kira listened carefully, but the muted scrape had subsided. Looking at Thomas, she shrugged and settled back to listen. She glanced at Jo and could see that the tyke's eyes were closed too, and she was forming the first words silently with her mouth.

The Singer held up one arm, and Kira, from her knowledge of the robe, knew that he was displaying the sleeve with the scene of the world's origin: the separation of land and sea, the emergence of fish and birds, all of it in the tiniest stitches around the border of the left sleeve, aloft now with his arm out-stretched. She could feel the awed admiration of the audience as they saw the robe displayed for the first time in a year, and she felt pride in the work she had done.

He started in a strong, rich baritone voice. No melody, yet, really. The Song began with a chant. Gradually, melodies would enter, Kira recalled; some slow, soaring lyrical phrases, followed by other harsher phrases with a quick pulsating beat. But it emerged slowly, as the world had. The Song began with the origin of the world, so many centuries before:

"In the beginning..."

20

Thomas nudged her and gestured with his head. Kira glanced over and smiled to see Jo, so eager and squirming earlier, now sound asleep in the big chair.

It was late morning and the Song had continued for several hours. Probably many of the tykes in the large hall were dozing, as Jo was.

Kira was surprised not to be bored and drowsy herself. But for her, the Song was also a journey through the patterned folds, and as the Singer sang, holding up the related parts, she remembered each scene and the days of work, the search through Annabella's threads for exactly the right shades. Though she remained attentive, occasionally her mind wandered to her own task that loomed ahead. Now that the old dyer's threads were almost gone — and the woman herself was gone too — Kira found herself desperately hoping that she would be able to remember and to create the dyes alone. Thomas drilled her again and again from his written pages.

Though Kira had told no one, not even Thomas, she had realized recently, to her surprise, that she could read many of the words. Watching his finger on the page one day, she had noticed that *goldenrod* and *greenwood* began the same way, with a looping downward curve. And they ended the same way too, with a little twiglike upright line. It was like a game, to find the marks that made the sounds. A forbidden game to be sure, but Kira found herself puzzling over it often when Thomas wasn't watching, and the puzzles had begun to explain themselves to her.

The Singer was in a quiet section now, one of those times following a great world disaster in which ice — white and gray sheets of it, made with small stitches so that it had no texture but instead an eerie, glistening smoothness — had engulfed the villages. Kira saw ice very seldom, only occasionally in the very coldest months when sleet struck the village, breaking tree branches, and the river froze near its banks. But she had remembered the fearsomeness and destruction of it when she worked on that section and had felt glad when beyond the edges of the ice disaster, green seeped in again and a quiet, fruitful time ensued.

He slid into the singing of the green part now, melodic and soothing, a relief after the frigid destruction that had made his voice harsh and forbidding.

Thomas leaned over and nudged her again. She glanced at Jo but the tyke had not moved. "Look down the aisle on the right," Thomas whispered.

She did, and saw nothing.

"Keep watching," Thomas murmured.

The Singer's voice continued. Kira watched the

side aisle. Suddenly she saw it: something moving stealthily, slowly, stopping now and then, and waiting; then creeping forward again.

People's heads blocked her view. Kira leaned slightly to the right, trying to see around them, trying not to let the Council of Guardians know that something disruptive was happening. She glanced at them but they were all attentive and focused on the Singer.

It moved again in the shadows, and she could see now that it was human, a small human, on all fours like a stalking beast. She could see too that people sitting on the edge of the aisle were beginning to notice, though they kept their eyes toward the stage. There was a very small stir; shoulders turning slightly, quick glances, expressions of surprise. The small human crept forward again, inching stealthily closer to the first row.

As he approached, it was easier for Kira to watch without changing her position, since her chair faced the audience, away from the stage. Finally, as the intruder reached the edge of the first row, he stopped creeping, squatted, and looked forward toward the stage — toward Kira, Jo, and Thomas — with a grin. Kira's heart leaped.

Matt! She didn't dare to speak aloud but she mouthed the word silently.

He wiggled his fingers in a wave.

The Singer inched his fingers up the staff, feeling for the place, and continued.

Matt grinned and opened one hand to show her

something. But the light was dim; Kira didn't recognize what he held. He held it up between his thumb and finger, displaying it to her importantly. She shook her head slightly, indicating that she couldn't tell what it was. Then, feeling guilty at her lapse in attention, she turned and began to watch the stage and the Singer again. Soon, she knew, there would be an intermission — a break for lunch. She would figure out a way to catch up with the tyke then, and examine and admire whatever he had brought.

Kira listened to the Singer's voice as he sang the serene melody of plentiful harvests and celebratory feasting. This part of the Song coincided with her own feelings at the moment. She experienced an enormous sense of relief and joy, now that Matt had returned and was safe.

When she looked back, he had crept away again, and the aisle was empty.

"May the little Singer have lunch with Thomas and me?"

It was the midday interruption of the Gathering, a lengthy gap in the day for food and rest. The tender pondered Kira's question and agreed. Leaving by the side door through which they had entered, Kira and Thomas, accompanied by Jo, yawning, went up the stairs to Kira's room and waited for their food to be brought. On the plaza outside, the people would be eating the food they had brought with them and discussing the Song. They would be anticipating the next section, a time of warfare, conflict, and death. Kira remembered it: the bright splatters of blood in crimson threads. But she put it out of her mind now.

While Thomas and Jo began on the large lunch that appeared on a tray, she hurried across the hall to Thomas's room to look down from the window and scan the crowd for a dirty-faced tyke and a bent-tailed dog.

But there was no need to search from the window. They were waiting for her in Thomas's room.

"Matt!" Kira cried. She set her stick aside, sat on the bed, and took him into her arms. Branch danced at her feet, his eager nose and tongue damp on her ankles.

"I been on a horrid long journey," Matt told her proudly.

She sniffed and smiled. "And you never washed, not *once*, while you were gone."

"There be no time for washing," he scoffed.

"I brung you a giftie," he told her eagerly, his eyes dancing with excitement.

"What was it that you held up at the Gathering? I couldn't see it."

"I brung you two things. A big and a little. The big be coming still. But I gots the little here in my pockie." He dug one hand deep into his pocket and pulled out a handful of nuts and a dead grasshopper.

"Nope. Be the other side." Matt put the grasshopper on the floor for Branch, who grabbed it with his teeth and consumed it with a crunch that made Kira cringe. The nuts rolled under the bed. Matt plunged his hand into the opposite pocket and brought out something triumphantly.

"Here you be!" He handed the thing to her.

She took the folded thing curiously and plucked the dead leaf pieces and dirt away. Then, while Matt watched with delight and pride suffusing his face, she unfolded it and held it to the window light. A square of filthy, wrinkled cloth. Nothing more. And yet it was everything.

"Matt!" Kira said, her voice hushed with awe. "You found blue!"

He beamed. "It were there, where she said."

"Where who said?"

"She. The old woman who makened the colors. She said there be blue yonder." He wiggled in excitement.

"Annabella? Yes, I remember. She *did* say that." Kira smoothed the cloth on the table, examining it. The deep blue was rich and even. The color of sky, of peace. "But how did you know where, Matt? How did you know where to go?"

He shrugged, grinning. "I recollect she pointed. I just followed where her point went. There be a path. But it's horrid far."

"And dangerous, Matt! It's through the woods!"

"There be nought fearful in the woods."

There be no beasts, Annabella had said.

187

"Me and Branchie, we walk for days and days. Branch, he et bugs. And me, I had some food I tooken —"

"— from your mother."

He nodded, with a guilty look. "But it weren't enough. After it be all gone, I et nuts, mostly.

"I could've et bugs if I had to," he added, boasting.

Kira half listened to his tale as she continued to smooth the cloth in her hand. She had yearned so for blue. Now here it was, in her grasp.

"Then when I got to the place, them people, they give me food. They got lots."

"But not a bath," Kira teased.

Matt scratched his dirty knee with dignity and ignored her. "They was horrid surprised to see me come. But they give me plenty of food. Branchie too. They liked Branchie."

Kira looked down at the dog, asleep now at her feet, and nudged him affectionately with the tip of her sandal. "Of course they did. Everybody loves Branch. But, Matt —"

"What?"

"Who are they? The people who have blue?"

He lifted his thin shoulders and wrinkled his forehead in an expression of ignorance. "Dunno," he said. "Them be all broken, them people. But there be plenty of food. And it's quiet-like, and nice."

"What do you mean, broken?"

He gestured toward her twisted leg. "Like you.

Some don't walk good. Some be broken in other ways. Not all. But lots. Do you think it maken them quiet and nice, to be broken?"

Puzzled by his description, Kira didn't answer. *Pain makes you strong,* her mother had told her. She had not said *quiet,* or *nice.*

"Anyways," Matt went on, "them got blue, for certain sure."

"For certain sure," Kira repeated.

"I suppose you like me best now, aye?" He grinned at her, and she laughed and said she liked him best of all.

Matt pulled away from her, and went to the window. On tiptoe he peered down and then out. The crowds were still there but he seemed to be looking beyond them for something. He frowned.

"You like the blue?" he asked her.

"Matt," she said passionately, "I love the blue. Thank you."

"It be the small giftie. But the big one be coming soon," he told her. He continued watching through the window. "Not yet, though."

He turned to her. "Got food?" he asked. "Iffen I wash?"

They left Matt and Branch in Thomas's room when they were summoned back to the afternoon section of the Gathering. This time they were ushered in and took their seats with less formality; there was no need for the chief guardian to introduce them to the villagers.

But the Singer, looking refreshed after lunch and a rest, made a ceremonial entrance again. He held his Staff as he stood at the foot of the stage, and the audience applauded him in acknowledgement of his remarkable performance in the morning. His expression didn't change. It had not changed all day. No proud smile. He simply stood gazing with intensity at the populace, the people for whom the Song was an entire history, the story of their upheavals, failures, and mistakes, as well as the telling of new tries and hopes. Kira and Thomas applauded as well, and Jo, watching and imitating them, clapped her hands enthusiastically.

Through the noise of the applause, as the Singer turned and mounted the stairs to the stage, Kira glanced at Thomas. He had heard it too. The dull, dragging sound of metal. The same sound they had noticed in the morning before the Song began.

Kira looked around, puzzled. No one else seemed to notice the abrupt, heavy noise. The villagers were watching the Singer as he breathed deeply in preparation. He moved to the center of the stage, closed his eyes, and fingered the Staff, looking for the place. He swayed slightly.

There! She had heard it again. Then, almost by accident, just for a second, she glimpsed it. Suddenly Kira realized with horror what the sound was. But now there was only silence. And then the start of the Song.

21

"What's wrong, Kira? Tell me!" Thomas was following her up the stairs. The Gathering had finally
ended. Jo had been led away by tenders but not
before she had had an exhilarating moment of tri-
umph.

At the end of the long afternoon, when the audience stood and sang, in chorus with the Singer, the
magnificent "Amen. So be it" that always formed the
Song's conclusion, the Singer himself had beckoned
to little Jo. Though the tyke had wriggled and dozed
during the long hours, now she looked up at him
with eagerness, and when it was clear that he was
summoning her to join him, she scrambled down
from her chair and ran enthusiastically to the stage.
She stood by his side and beamed with satisfaction,
waving one small arm in the air, while the people,
released now from their solemnity, whistled and
stamped their feet in appreciation.

Kira, watching, remained motionless and silent,
overwhelmed with her new knowledge and a heavy
feeling that combined dread and terrible sorrow.

That fear and sadness stayed with her as she

limped laboriously upstairs and Thomas urged her to explain what was wrong. She took a deep breath and prepared herself to tell him what she knew.

But at the top of the staircase, they were interrupted by the sight of Matt in the corridor outside Kira's open door. He was grinning broadly and dancing impatiently from foot to foot.

"It's here!" Matt called. "The big giftie!"

Kira entered the room and stopped just inside the door. She stared curiously at the stranger who sat slumped wearily in her chair. She could tell from his long legs that the man was quite tall. There was gray in his hair, though he was not old; three syllables, she thought, trying to categorize him in some way that would perhaps explain his presence. Yes, three syllables, about the same as Jamison; maybe the age of her mother's brother, she decided.

She nudged Thomas. "Look," she whispered, indicating the color of the man's loose shirt. "*Blue.*"

The intruder stood and turned toward her at the sound of her voice and at the continued bursts of Matt's barely-contained excitement. Kira wondered briefly why he had not risen when she entered. It would have been the expected gesture for even the most inconsiderate or hostile stranger, and this man appeared to be both friendly and courteous. He was smiling slightly. But now she could see, to her distress, that he was blind. Scars crossed and disfigured his face with jagged lines across his forehead and down the length of one cheek, and his eyes were opaque and unseeing. She had never seen anyone with destroyed vision before, though she had heard of such things happening through accident or disease. But damaged people were useless; they were always taken to the Field.

Why was this sightless man alive? Where had Matt found him?

And why was he here?

Matt was still prancing about with anticipation. "I brung him!" he announced gleefully. He touched the man's hand and demanded confirmation. "I brung you, didn't I?"

"You did," the man said, and his voice was affectionate toward the tyke. "You were a wonderful guide. You brought me almost all the way."

"I brung him all the way from yonder!" Matt said, turning to Kira and Thomas. "But then at the end he wanted to feel his way alone. I be telling him he can keep Branchie for a helper, but he want to do it all alone. So he gimme the scrap for the first giftie. See?" Matt pulled at the man's shirt and showed Kira the hem, at the back, from which he had torn the piece of cloth.

"I'm sorry," Kira said politely to the man. She felt awkward and uncertain in his presence. "Your shirt is ruined."

"I have others," the man said with a smile. "He wanted so badly to show you the gift. And I felt a need to find my way by myself. I have been here before, but it was a long time ago."

"And look!" Matt was like a toddler or a puppy, dashing about in excitement. He picked up a bag from the floor beside the chair and pulled its drawstring open. "Now we be needing some water," he said, lifting several wilted plants out gently, "but these be all right. They be perking up when we give them a drinkie.

"But you never be guessing what!" Now he turned to the blind man again and tugged at his sleeve to be certain he was paying attention.

"What?" The man seemed amused.

"She gots water right here! You probably be thinking we gotta take these plants to the river! But right here, iffen I open this door, she gots water that squirts out!"

He pranced to the door and opened it.

"Take the plants, then, Matt," the man suggested, "and give them their drink."

He turned toward Kira and she could tell that he knew how to feel her presence in his darkness. "It's woad we've brought you," he explained. "It's the plant that my people use to make blue dye."

"Your beautiful shirt," she murmured, and he smiled again.

"Matt told me that it's the same shade as the sky on a sunny summer-start morning," he said.

Kira agreed. "Yes," she said. "That's it, exactly!"

"Much the same as the blossom on a morning glory vine, I would think," the man said.

194

"Yes, that's true! But how —"

"I haven't always been sightless. I remember those things."

They could hear the sound of running water. "Matt? Don't drown them!" the man called. "It would be a very long trip back to get more!"

He turned back to Kira. "I would be happy to bring more, of course. But I think you won't need that."

"Please," Kira said, "sit down. And we'll have a meal sent up. It's time for dinner anyway." Even in her confusion, she tried to remember the basic courtesies. The man had brought her a gift of great value. Why he had done it, she couldn't begin to comprehend. Nor how hard it must have been to come a great distance with no eyes and no guide but a lively boy and a bent-tailed dog.

And at the last of the journey, when Matt had run ahead with his treasured scrap of blue, the blind man had come alone. How was it possible?

"I'll call the tenders and tell them," Thomas said.

The man looked startled and concerned. "Who's that?" he asked, hearing Thomas's voice for the first time.

"I live down the hall," Thomas explained. "I carved the Singer's staff while Kira did the Robe. Maybe you don't understand about the Gathering, but it's just ended, and it's a really impor —"

"I know about it," the man said. "I know all about it.

"Please. Don't call for food," he added firmly. "No one must know that I'm here."

"Food?" Matt asked, emerging from the bathroom.

"I'll have them bring our dinners to my room down the hall, and no one will know," Thomas suggested. "We'll all share it. There's always more than enough."

Kira nodded agreement, and Thomas left the room to summon the tenders. Matt scampered behind him, alert to the prospect of food.

Now Kira found herself alone with the stranger in the blue shirt. She could tell from his posture that he was very tired. She sat down, facing him, on the edge of the bed and sought in her mind the right things to say to him, the right questions to ask.

"Matt's a good boy," she said after a moment's silence, "but he forgets some important things in his excitement. He didn't tell you my name. I'm Kira."

The blind man nodded. "I know. He told me all about you."

She waited. Finally, into the quiet, she said, "He didn't tell me who you are."

The man stared with his unseeing eyes into the room, beyond the place where Kira sat. He began to speak, faltered, took a breath, then stopped.

"It's beginning to get dark," he said finally. "I'm facing the window, and I can feel the change in daylight."

"Yes."

196

"It's how I found my way here after Matt left me at the edge of the village. We had planned to wait and arrive at night, in the darkness. But there were no people about, so it was safe for us to enter in daylight. Matt realized it was the day of the Gathering."

"Yes," Kira said. "It began very early in the morning." *He is not going to answer my question,* she thought.

"I remember the Gatherings. And I remembered the path. The trees have grown, of course. But I could feel the shadows. I could feel my way along the center of the path by the way the light fell."

He smiled wryly. "I could smell the butcher's hut."

Kira nodded and chuckled.

"And when I passed the weaving shed, I could smell the fabrics folded there, and even the wood of the looms.

"If the women had been at work, I would have recognized the sounds." With his tongue against the roof of his mouth, he made the repetitive muted clacking sound of the shuttle, and then the whisper of the threads turning into cloth.

"And so I made my way here all alone. Matt met me then and brought me to your room."

Kira waited. Then she asked, "Why?"

As she watched, he touched his own face. He ran his hand over the scars, feeling the edges; then he followed the jagged skin down the side of his own cheek, along his neck. Finally he reached into his blue

197

shirt and pulled forward the leather thong that hung there. As he held it in his hand, she saw the polished half-rock that matched her own.

"Kira," he said, but he did not need to tell her now, because she knew, "my name is Christopher. I'm your father."

In shock, she stared at him. She watched his ruined eyes, and saw that they were able, still, to weep.

22

In some hidden place to which Matt had led him in the night, her father slept. But before he had left her in order to sleep, he had told her his story.

"No, it was not beasts," he said, in reply to her first questions. "It was men.

"There are no beasts out there," he said. His voice was as certain as Annabella's had been. *There be no beasts.*

"But —" Kira began to interrupt, to tell her father what Jamison had told her. *I saw your father taken by beasts,* Jamison had said. But she waited and continued to listen.

"Oh, there are wild creatures in the forest, of course. We hunted them for food. We still do. Deer. Squirrel. Rabbit." He sighed. "It was a large hunt that day. The men had gathered for the distribution of weapons. I had a spear and a sack of food. Katrina had prepared food for me. She always did."

"Yes, I know," Kira whispered.

He seemed not to hear her. With his blank eyes he seemed to be looking backward in time. "She was expecting a child," he said, smiling. He gestured with his hand, making a curve in the air above his own belly. In a dreamlike way, Kira felt herself, small, inside the curve made by his arched fingers, inside the memory of her mother.

"We went in the usual way: together at first, in groups, then separating into pairs, and eventually finding ourselves alone as we followed tracks or sounds deeper into the forest."

"Were you frightened?" Kira asked.

He shook himself loose from the slow measured speech of his memory, and smiled. "No, no. There was no danger. I was an accomplished hunter. One of the best. I was never frightened in the forest."

Then his brow furrowed. "I should have been wary, though. I knew that I had enemies. There were jealousies, always, and there were rivals. It was a way of life here. Perhaps it still is."

Kira nodded. Then she remembered that he couldn't see her acknowledgement. "Yes," she told him. "It still is."

"I was soon to be appointed to the Council of Guardians," he went on. "It was a job with great power. Others wanted the post. I suppose it was that. Who knows? There was always hostility here. Harsh words. I haven't thought about it in a long time, but now I recall the arguments and anger — even that morning, when the weapons were assigned —"

Kira told him, "It happened again recently, at the beginning of a hunt. I saw it. Fights and arguing. It's always that way. It's the way of men."

He shrugged. "So it hasn't changed."

"How could it change? It's the way it is. It's what tykes are taught, to grab and shove. It's the only way people can get what they want. I would have been taught that way too, but for my leg," Kira said.

"Your leg?"

He didn't know. How could he?

Now she felt embarrassed, having to tell him. "It's twisted. I was born that way. They wanted to take me to the Field but my mother said no."

"She defied them? Katrina?" His face lit and he smiled. "And she won!"

"Her father was still alive, and he was a person of great importance, she told me. And so they let her keep me. They probably thought I would die anyway."

"But you were strong."

"Yes. Mother said pain made me strong." Telling him, she was no longer embarrassed, but proud, and she wanted him to be proud, too.

He reached out, and she took his hand.

She wanted him to go on. She needed to know what had happened. She waited.

"I don't know for certain who it was," he explained when he continued. "I can guess, of course. I knew he was bitterly envious. Apparently he approached silently behind me, and as I waited there, watching for the deer I'd been stalking, he attacked me; first with a club to my head, so that I was stunned and dazed, and then with his knife. He left me for dead."

"But you lived. You were strong." Kira squeezed his hand.

"I woke in the Field. I suppose draggers had taken me there and left me, as they do. You've been to the Field?"

Kira nodded, then remembered his blindness again, and said it aloud. "Yes." She would have to tell him when and why. But not yet.

"I would have died there, as I was supposed to. I couldn't move, couldn't see. I was dazed and in great pain. I *wanted* to die.

"But that night," he went on, "strangers came to the Field.

"I thought at first that it was diggers. I tried to tell them that I was still alive. But when they spoke, it was with the voice of strangers. They used our language, but with a different lilt, a slight change of cadence. Even as desperately wounded as I was, I could hear the difference. And their voices were soothing. Gentle. They held something to my mouth, a drink made of herbs. It dulled my pain and made me sleepy. They placed me on a carrying litter they had made of thick branches —"

"Who were they?" Kira asked, fascinated, unable to keep from interrupting.

"I didn't know. I couldn't see them. My eyes were destroyed and I was almost delirious with pain. But I could hear their comforting voices. So I drank the liquid and gave myself up to their care."

Kira was astonished. In her entire lifetime in the village, she had never encountered a single person who would have done such a thing. She knew no one who would be willing to soothe or comfort or aid a grievously wounded being. Or who would know *how.*

Except Matt, she thought, remembering how the boy had nursed his little damaged dog back to life.

"They carried me a very great distance through the forest," her father went on. "It took several days. I woke and slept and woke again. Each time I woke, they talked to me, cleaned me, gave me water to drink, and more of the drug to ease my pain.

"Everything was blurred. I didn't remember what had happened or why. But they healed me, as much as I could be healed, and they told me the truth: I would never see again. But they told me also that they would help me to make a life without sight."

"But who *were* they?" Kira asked again.

"Who *are* they, you should say," he told her gently, "because they still exist. And I am one of them now.

"They were just people. But they are people like me, who were damaged. Who had been left to die."

"Who had been taken from our village to the Field?"

Her father smiled. "Not only from here. There are other places. They had come from all over, those who had been wounded — sometimes not just in body, but in other ways as well. Some traveled very long distances. It's astounding to hear of the difficult journeys.

"And those who had reached this place where I found myself? They had formed their own community — my community now, too —"

Kira remembered what Matt had described, a place where broken people lived.

"They help each other," her father explained simply. "*We* help each other.

"Those who can see? They guide me. I am never without helping eyes.

"Those who can't walk? They are carried."

Kira unconsciously rubbed her own damaged leg.

"There is always someone to lean on," he told her. "Or a pair of strong hands for those who have none.

"The village of the healing has existed for a long time," he explained. "Wounded people still come. But now it is beginning to change, because children have been born there and are growing up. So we have strong, healthy young people among us. And we have others who have found us and stayed because they wanted to share our way of life."

Kira was trying to picture it. "So it is a village, like this one?"

"Much the same. We have gardens. Houses. Families. But it is much quieter than this village. There is no arguing. People share what they have, and help each other. Babies rarely cry. Children are cherished."

Kira looked at the stone pendant that rested against his blue shirt. She touched her own matching one.

"Do you have a family there?" she asked hesitantly.

"The whole village is like a family to me, Kira," he replied. "But I have no wife, no child. Is that what you mean?"

"Yes."

"I left my family here. Katrina and the child to come." He smiled. "You."

She knew she must tell him now.

"Katrina —" she began.

"I know. Your mother is dead. Matt told me."

Kira nodded, and for the first time in many months she began to cry for her own loss. She had not wept when her mother died. She had willed herself to be strong then, to decide what to do and to do it. Now hot tears stained her face and she covered it with her hands. Her shoulders shook as she sobbed. Her father opened his arms, offering her an embrace, but she turned from him.

"Why didn't you come back?" she asked finally, choking on the words as she tried to stop crying.

Looking out through the shield she had made with her hands over her eyes, she could see that the question pained him.

"For a very long time," he said at last, "I remembered nothing. The blows to my head had been intended to kill me, though they failed. But they took my memory. Who I was, why I was there? My wife? My home? I knew nothing of any of it.

"Then, very slowly, as I healed, it began to come back. I remembered small things of the past. Your mother's voice. A song she sang, *'Night comes, and colors fade away; sky fades, for blue can never stay . . .'*"

Startled by the familiar lullaby, Kira murmured the words with him. "Yes," she whispered. "I remember it too."

"Then very gradually, it all came back to me. But I could not return. I didn't know how to find the way. I was blind and weakened.

"And if I did find a way back, it would be to meet my death. The ones who wanted me dead were still here.

"Finally," he explained, "I simply stayed. I mourned my losses. But I stayed and made a life there, without your mother. Without you.

"And then," he went on, his expression lightening, "after so many years had gone by, the boy appeared. He was exhausted when he arrived, and hungry."

"He's always hungry," Kira said, smiling slightly.

"He said he had come all that way because he had heard that we had blue. He wanted blue for his special friend, who had learned to make all the other colors. When he told me about you, Kira, I knew you

206

must be my daughter. I knew I must let him lead me back."

He stretched slightly, and yawned. "The boy will find me a safe place to sleep when he returns."

Kira took his hand, and held it. There were scars even there, she saw.

"Father," she said, feeling her way uncertainly with the word she had never used before, "they won't hurt you now."

"No, I'll be safely hidden. And after I'm rested, we will slip away, you and I. The boy will help us pack food for the journey. You will be my eyes on the way home. And I will be the strong legs you lean on."

"No, Father!" Kira said, excited now. "Look!" She waved her arm, indicating the comfortable room. Then she paused, embarrassed. "I'm sorry. I know you can't really look. But you can *feel* how comfortable it is. There are other rooms like it along the hall, all of them empty except the ones where Thomas and I live. One can be readied for you."

He was shaking his head. "No," he said.

"You don't understand, Father, because you've not been here, but I have a special role in the village. And because of it, I have a special friend on the Council of Guardians. He saved my life! And he looks after me.

"Oh, it's too much to explain, and I know you're tired. But Father, not very long ago, I was in great danger. Someone named Vandara wanted me to be put to the Field. There was a trial. And —"

"Vandara? I remember her. That's the scarred woman?"

"Yes, that's the one," Kira acknowledged.

"It was a terrible thing, her injury. I remember when it happened. She blamed her child. He slipped on wet rocks and grabbed her skirt, so that she fell and gashed her chin and neck on a sharp rock.

"But I thought —"

"He was only a small tyke, but she blamed him. Later, when he died, from the oleander, there were questions. Some people suspected —" He paused, and sighed. "But there was no proof of her guilt.

"She's a cruel woman, though," Kira's father said. "You say she turned on you? And there was a trial?"

"Yes, but I was allowed to stay. I was even given an honored place. I had a defender, a guardian named Jamison. And now he looks after me, Father, and supervises my work. I know he'll find a place for you!"

Happily Kira squeezed her father's hand, thinking of the future they would have together. But it was as if the air in the room shifted. Lines in her father's face tightened. The hand that she held stiffened and withdrew from hers.

"Your defender. Jamison?" Her father touched his own scarred face again. "Yes, he tried to find a place for me before. Jamison is the one who tried to kill me."

23

Alone in the dim pre-dawn moonlight of not-yet morning, Kira went down to the dyer's garden that had been so carefully created for her. There, gently patting earth around the moist roots, she planted the woad. "'Gather fresh leaves from first year's growth of woad.'" She repeated the words that Annabella had said. "'And soft rainwater; that makes the blue.'" She carried water from a container in the shed, and soaked the soil around the fragile plants. It would be a long time until the first year's growth. She would not be here to gather those leaves.

When the plants were watered, she sat alone, knees to chin, and rocked herself back and forth as the sun began to rise, a faint pink stain creeping up the eastern rim of the sky. The village was still silent. She tried to put it all together in her mind, to make some sense of it.

But there was no sense, no meaning at all.

Her mother's death: a sudden violent, isolated illness. Such things were rare. Usually illness struck the village and many were taken.

Perhaps her mother had posioned?

But why?

Because they wanted Kira.

Why?

So that they could capture her gift: her skill with the threads.

And Thomas? His parents too? And Jo's?

Why?

So that all their gifts would be captive.

Despairing, Kira stared through the early dawn at the garden. The plants glimmered and shifted in the breeze, some of them still in autumn-start bloom. Now, finally, woad had been added to give her the blue she had yearned for. But someone else would harvest the first leaves.

Somewhere nearby, her father slept, gathering strength to return with his newfound daughter to the village where healing people lived in harmony. Together he and Kira would steal away and leave the only world she had ever known. She looked forward to the journey. She would not miss the squalor and noise they would leave behind.

She would long for Matt and his mischief, she thought sadly. And Thomas, so serious and dedicated; she would miss him, too.

And Jo. She smiled at the thought of the little singer who had waved so proudly to the crowd at the Gathering.

Thinking of Jo, Kira remembered something. In the confusion and excitement of her father's arrival, it had disappeared from her mind. Now the awareness and the horror came back, and she gasped.

The muted clanking sound that had puzzled her during the celebration! She could almost hear it again in her mind, a dragging of metal. She had glimpsed its cause at the beginning of the second half of the Song. Then at the conclusion, after the Singer had acknowledged the people's applause, after Jo had scampered happily down from the stage, he moved toward the steps to descend and walk down the aisle. He lifted the robe slightly at the top of the steps, and from her seat at the edge of the stage Kira saw his feet. They were bare and grotesquely misshapen.

His ankles were thickly scarred, more damaged than her father's face. They were caked and scabbed with dried blood. Fresh, bright blood trickled in narrow rivulets across his feet. It all came from the raw, festering skin — infected and dripping — around the metal cuffs with which he was bound. Between the thick ankle cuffs, dragging heavily as he made his way slowly from the stage, was a chain.

He lowered the robe then, and she saw nothing more. Perhaps, she thought, she had imagined it? But watching him as he moved, she heard the sound of the scraping chain against the floor, and she could see behind him a smeared, darkened trail of his blood.

Recalling it now, Kira knew, suddenly and with clarity, what it all meant. It was so simple.

The three of them — the new little Singer who would one day take the chained Singer's place; Thomas the Carver, who with his meticulous tools

211

wrote the history of the world; and she herself, the one who colored that history — they were the artists who could create the future.

Kira could feel it in her fingertips: her ability to twist and weave the colors into the scenes of amazing beauty that she had made all alone, before they assigned her the task of the robe. Thomas had told her that once he too had carved astonishing things into wood that seemed to come alive in his hands. And she could hear the high, haunting melody that the child had sung in her magical voice, solitary in her room, before they had forced her from it and given her their own song to sing.

The guardians with their stern faces had no creative power. But they had strength and cunning, and they had found a way to steal and harness other people's powers for their own needs. They were forcing the children to describe the future they wanted, not the one that could be.

Kira watched the garden tremble and move as it slept. She saw the newly planted woad settle in, nestled where she had laid it gently beside the yellow bedstraw. "Mostly it dies after flowering once," Annabella had said, describing woad. "But sometimes you find a small shoot lives."

It was those small living shoots she had planted, and something in Kira knew without a doubt that they would survive. She knew something else as well, and with the realization, she rose from the damp grass to go indoors, to find her father and tell him that she could not be his eyes. That she must stay.

Matt was the one who would lead Christopher home.

Late at night they gathered, at the edge of the path that led away from the village, the same path that would wind past Annabella's clearing and continue onward for days to the village of the healing people. Matt was prancing about, eager to begin the journey, proud of his role as the leader. Branch, also eager to set off on an adventure, sniffed and wandered here and there.

"I know you be missing me horrid," Matt confided, "and maybe I be gone a long time, because maybe they be wanting me to visit."

He turned to Christopher. "They gots plenty of food all the time? For visitors? And doggies?"

Christopher, smiling, nodded yes.

Then Matt took Kira aside to whisper an important secret. "I know you can't be getting a hubby because of your horrid gimp," he said in a low, apologetic voice.

"It's all right," she reassured him.

He tugged at her sleeve eagerly. "I been wanting to tell you that them other people — them broken ones? They gets married. And I seen a boy there, a two-syllable boy, not even broken, just about the same age as you.

"I bet you could marry him," Matt announced in

a solemn whisper, "iffen you want to."

Kira hugged him. "Thanks, Matt," she whispered back. "I don't want to."

"His eyes be a very amazing blue," Matt said importantly, as if it might matter.

But Kira smiled and shook her head no.

Thomas carried the bundle of food they had saved and packed; there, at the beginning of the path, he transferred it to Christopher's strong back. Then the two shook hands.

Kira waited silently.

Her father understood her decision. "You will come when you can," he said to her. "Matt will go back and forth. He will be our tie. And one day he will bring you."

"One day our villages will know each other," Kira assured him. "I can feel that already." It was true. She could feel the future through her hands, in the pictures her hands were urging her to make. She could feel the broad undecorated expanse waiting, across the shoulders of the robe.

"I have a gift for you," her father told her.

She looked at him, puzzled. He had come empty-handed and had lived in hiding for the past few days. But now he put something soft into her hands, something that had a quality of comfort.

She could sense but could not see, in the darkness, what it was.

"Threads?" she asked. "A bundle of threads?"

Her father smiled. "I had time, sitting alone,

while I waited to return. And my hands are very clever because they have learned to do things unseeing.

"Bit by bit I unraveled the fabric of my blue shirt," he explained. "The boy found me another to wear."

"I filched it," Matt announced with matter-of-fact pride.

"So you will have blue threads," her father went on, "while you wait for your plants to come to life."

"Goodbye," Kira whispered, and hugged her father. She watched through the darkness as the blind man, the renegade boy, and the bent-tailed dog set off down the path. Then, when she could see them no longer, she turned and walked back to what lay waiting. The blue was gathered in her hand, and she could feel it quiver, as if it had been given breath and was beginning to live.